Flashbulb Memories

by

John Kemp

Published in 2015 by JK Publishing
Revised in 2024 by JK Publishing
Copyright © John Kemp Author
Copyright © Michelle Parrish-Kemp, John Kemp: Cover Book Design

The author or authors assert their moral right under the Copyright, Designs, and Patents Act, 1988, to be identified as the author or authors of this work.

All Rights reserved. No part of this publication may be reproduced, copied, stored in a retrieval system, or transmitted, in any form or by any means, without the prior written consent of the copyright holder, nor be otherwise circulated in any form of binding or cover other than that in which it is published and without a similar condition being imposed on the subsequent purchaser.

A CIP catalogue record for this title is available from the British Library.

In this work of fiction, the characters, places and events are either the product of the author's imagination or they are used entirely fictitiously.

Also by John Kemp

Film Noirs and Mini Bars
Film Noirs and Spanish Guitars
Film Noirs and Pullman Cars
Film Noirs and Doused Cigars (2024)

Far Reaching Aspects
Vanished into Thin Air
The Secret Letterbox
Ten Strands
Pool of Deceit
Trouble in Bath

www.johnkempauthor.com

Credit and Thanks to:

Emily LeVault for Copyediting and Developmental Editing, 2024 version. Emily L @elevault200 on Fiverr

Gabriel Bayes for editing the 2015 version.
Michelle for cover layout and design.
Julia for your feedback 2015
Steve of FeedARead 2015
Charlie of eBook Pioneers 2015

Cover Photo Credits:

Brass locket by Horiyan
Forget-me-not (flower) by Oksana 2010
Artist's impression of the Battle of Britain by Keith Tarrier
Rolling countryside around a farm by Kevin Eaves
Woman in black & white by Kaponia Aliaksei
Frame wallpaper torn (with vintage brown background) A Banana Republic Image

All images from Shutterstock.com
Cover design, Graphics & Photoshop: Michelle Parrish-Kemp, John Kemp.

A flashbulb memory is a highly detailed, exceptionally vivid 'snapshot' of the moment and circumstances in which a piece of surprising and consequential (or emotionally arousing) news was experienced or heard.

The term "Flashbulb memory" suggests the surprise, indiscriminate illumination, detail, and brevity of a photograph; however, flashbulb memories are only somewhat indiscriminate and are far from complete.

Evidence has shown that although people are highly confident in their memories, the details of the memories can be forgotten.

Courtesy of Wikipedia

~For Joy~

~Prologue~

My recurring flashbulb memory: A village somewhere in England.

A damp fog - rather than a right 'pea-souper' as my friend Harry used to say - hangs just above the slated rooftops, shrouding a row of chimney pots. Shoe-box gardens run the full length of a street of Victorian terraces.

I see my hand on a brass knocker before closing the front door to one of these houses.

The air is sharp and my breath is visible. I glance down at my heavy boots, which scuff against the flagstones. A kitbag swings from one shoulder, my rifle on the other, and an ammunition pouch is wrapped around my waist.

I turn my face towards the faint glow of the morning sun and pause before buttoning up my army jacket, lighting my last roll up. I inhale, lost in thought, and survey the house before leaving: its dirty windows, its sloping roof and the grey chimney stacks; home.

I pick up my haversack and the little iron-gate squeaks as I pull it closed behind me.

I walk a short distance, stopping at a little tobacconist off the village square. The bell above the door jangles and an elderly man appears from the back of the house. He has a grey handlebar moustache, wears round spectacles and is almost bald. I buy a packet of Woodbines.

'Sixpence change, sir.' The man gives me a kindly smile.

I nod in gratitude.

'Good luck over there.'

'Thanks.'

'You'll be back in Blighty before you know it.'

I bid him a farewell and he waves a cheerio, adding, 'God bless you sir,' and he disappears behind the curtain once again.

Outside, the fog soon lifts and a misty rain ensues as I walk on to the railway station.

While a brass band plays, soldiers smoke, chat and say their goodbyes to their loved ones.

I squeeze through the door of 'The Station Cafe' to meet a young woman. I smell her perfume; stroke her hair and we kiss. I am unable to see her full face, but I feel the release of her hand and she is gone, lost in the chaos and smoke and steam from the train.

One blast of a shrill whistle signals embarkation; the carriage doors are flung open and we pile in.

Soon soldiers are bagging seats, stowing kitbags, gas capes and respirators behind them and throwing their haversacks onto the racks above.

The guard blows his whistle and the train pulls out. Most of the men are still jostling for position and there is much rancour, grumbling and general disorder.

Less than a mile down the track, we hear the drone of enemy aircraft, then a roar as they pass just overhead. In the carriages, to a soldier, we pause when we hear the sound of bombs being dropped upon our village...

These are the bare bones of my existing memory.

~Part 1~

~Chapter 1~

Six months later, Bournemouth

1st August, 1944

Coughing, cries for assistance and weary groans are my recent company; no-one laughs or smiles in my ward, rarely at least; some have not even made it out alive.

I cry silent tears as I view the lifeless bodies being taken away. The poor light from the few small windows causes day and night to blur, and only the dim evening lamps tell me another day is ending. In a vain effort to sleep, I try to ignore the putrid smell of idoform and shut out those wretched noises.

I am one of the lucky ones from the D-Day landings, or so everyone keeps telling me. I have to believe them since I have survived to return home to British soil from Occupied France. After a blood transfusion and surgery, I am surprised to be alive. So, for me, it's like having an unexpected second inning.

'How did your regiment get on over there?' I ask a fellow patient.

'A grim business,' he says and solemnly shakes his head. 'There were heavy casualties in my regiment; many didn't make it off the beach. I lost so many friends and colleagues. The Germans had reinforced their defences... Slowly but surely, we were able to make headway but it was hard-going...'

6th August, 1944

I have been moved to a different wing, a smaller ward, one where the patients are in recovery.

Here, there are huge, long shuttered windows, lofty ceilings and dark parquet floors. Two rows of fifteen beds line each side of the ward. All manner of staff come and go. Recently, we even had a visit from top brass; a brigadier came through and gave us all a few quiet words of encouragement.

My new bed is close to a small office from where I can sometimes hear the hushed sound of the nurse's chatter.

Yesterday, when the door was inadvertently left ajar, I could hear a radio. The blissful musical tones escaped and floated towards me. I recognised the composition: Where the Lemon Trees Bloom by Johann Strauss. I gazed out of the window as the music washed over me, cleansing my soul so that I forgot the present.

The duty nurses are worried about me. Twice during their crossover, I have caught Nurse Grant and Nurse Brooks glancing towards me through the small office window. I could not hear their whispered conversations or decipher their furtive glances, but I could sense they were talking about me.

Intuitively, I know it concerns my previous designated stay in a secure room of the hospital.

~Chapter 2~

Hospital staff tell me I was in a coma for nearly six weeks, but I am making progress.

Presently, each day, after breakfast, I am pushed through a draughty room with high ceilings and leaky radiators to my rehabilitation class. This involves a series of basic exercises that a small child could do, but mostly I cannot. There are about twenty of us crammed in there, some in wheelchairs, some needing walking frames, most slumped down in hardback chairs.

I turn my stiff neck to see the human debris of war all around me. Men are empty shells of their former selves; some stare into space or even fall into a semi-conscious state.

We begin by throwing a football to each other; some progress to a medicine ball. An ironic cheer goes up on the rare occasion that a patient completes a successful throw. The nurse is a good sport and retrieves the ball more times than any third-rate, amateur goalkeeper.

My constant fumbling of the ball reminds me of how my life has changed; my spirit has been crushed, as has that of my colleagues. War does that to you; it first crushes you physically and then mentally. When you are no longer fit to be a soldier, you end up in places like this.

I presume that hospitals up and down the country must be full of us by now, doing stuff like this, and simply surviving, no more and no less. On the good days, I do have hope…

You see, amidst these tortured souls, there are angels who watch over us.

To be honest, I am not sure how these angels do it, but they do, and for seemingly no reward. What they see, and what they hear must be extraordinarily testing because we are not good patients, and no kind of training can prepare anyone for this. My thoughts are interrupted.

'Cup of tea?' A kitchen orderly asks and stops the trolley at the foot of my bed.

I raise a thumb.

'You all right today?' she asks as she pours.

'Mustn't grumble,' I reply.

'There you go, love,' she smiles. 'Careful now, it's hot.'

'Thank you,' I say and reflect upon this seemingly simple offering.

Tea: what would we do without it, particularly after a disappointment or a tragedy? It is often offered in kindness or sympathy to stress that everything will somehow be all right. 'Don't you worry; keep your chin up; have a cup of tea; keep calm and carry on.'

And do you know what? It does help. As I sip my hot tea, I gradually relax and am refreshed. To my mind, the 'tea lady' has one of the most important jobs in the whole war effort.

Anyway, where was I? Ah yes...

My favourite angel is an assistant called Nurse Brooks. I sense (or at least I want to believe) that she has taken a keen interest in me. When I say 'interest', I mean she spends time talking with me. If I am awake late at night, she will sometimes pull up a chair and chat for a while. Giving too much attention to one patient might elicit the wrath of the stalking Matron. I hope not, because Nurse Brooks is the only light in my new existence.

Matron is a tough, old boot; durable, hardy, and a bit frayed. Her eyes exhibit little sentiment but they detect errors and apathy amongst the staff like a swooping hawk. She walks with a straight back and a chin that is rarely lowered. If she has ever smiled, I have never been a witness to it.

During the day, whenever Nurse Brooks is on duty, I raise my head slightly so my eyes can follow her around the ward. She wears a standard issue, striped, blue dress with a white collar and a starched white apron with a cotton mob cap, one that covers her pretty brown hair. I suppose, for most, this would be very unflattering garb.

In a similar way to those dulcet sounds coming from the radio, seeing her lifts my spirits and gives me hope. I watch as the nurses give the first of many penicillin injections. Later on, Nurse Brooks pushes a dressing cart and, together with Nurse Gibbs, dresses the wounds of patients.

Nurse Brooks always senses me watching her, because on occasion she has turned around and given me a secret smile or an exclusive wink. I confess that one night I even dreamt that she was lying next to me...she has frequently encouraged me to recall my flashbulb memory, cajoling me to remember more and to help me find my past.

Even a few minutes of sitting up in bed, however, can be too much, and I soon flop back down and leave Nurse Brooks to her duties.

Aside from that, the days that pass here are slow and indistinguishable. Breakfast follows exercise, lunch follows the nurses' rounds or the Matron's inspections, and drug-induced sleep follows everything.

~Chapter 3~

In Recovery, 2nd September, 1944

I have already surmised that Nurse Brooks is not married, but she has cleverly deflected my casual, and then not-so-casual, questions about any current relationships during her check-ups with me.

'You're doing better,' she laughs.

'What do you say?' I ask (regarding my latest proposition).

'There's a war on,' she says, roughly sticking a thermometer in my mouth. 'I haven't got the time for romantic notions like that.'

'Besides, I'm very discerning,' she adds, not looking up as she makes a note of the reading.

When I suggest we go for a coffee, she sticks the damn thermometer back in my mouth. 'One more time,' she requests, and playfully stops me in my tracks because I know that one reading is de rigueur, but she finally yields.

'Okay.' She sighs deeply and removes the thermometer. 'When all of this is over, and when you're fully recovered.'

'Is that a promise?'

'Oh, if only to stop you feeling sorry for yourself,' she says and severely re-arranges the pillows behind my head. 'Okay, yes.'

Before I have time to enjoy the moment, Matron is upon us.

'How are you today?' Matron asks. 'Your shoulder?'

'Oh, I'm quite all right. The stabbing pain has gone.' I glance to Nurse Brooks and smile. 'Actually, thanks to my angel here, I'm in heaven, Matron.'

Matron scoffs and gives Nurse Brooks a stony glance.

'Ignore him, Matron,' she says. 'He's just in high spirits.'

'Very well.' She nods. 'I daresay that is down to you, but don't forget your other patients. Carry on nurse.'

As Matron moves on, I give a theatrical shivering motion. 'There's suddenly a cold draught in here.'

Nurse Brooks nervously places a finger to her mouth. 'Shh... She takes a dim view on any banter between nurses and patients.'

'She would. She's a wet blanket.'

'You can't say things like that.'

'Oh, I was just pulling her leg a bit.'

'If she thought you were fraternising with me, she would have me removed from the ward. I could even lose my position. Then you wouldn't see me at all.' She sighs, 'Do you want that?'

'Of course not. That's the last thing I want to happen. I'll be a bit more careful,' I promise.

'Anyway, did you really mean that?'

'What - you being an angel? Absolutely! You are an angel.'

Nurse Brooks' expression is stoic, but her lips upturn in the merest hint of satisfaction.

'Nursing is hard sometimes; I am doing my best.'

'You are the best!'

'Okay, that's enough,' she directs. 'You do know where all this flattery will get you?'

'Where?' I ask, hopeful.

'Nowhere!'

I shrug. 'Well, you can't blame a fellow for trying.'

'No,' she scoffs. 'But I'll give you full marks for effort.'

When Nurse Brooks begins pouring me a cup of water, I return to the topic in hand and try my luck further.

'If I promise to behave in here, then perhaps we could have dinner together?'

'Hey!' She stops pouring. 'It was just a coffee a minute ago.'

I shrug. 'Coffee after dinner.'

She places the jug down.

'Jack... I should tell you, I have certain criteria.'

'What sort of criteria?' I ask sincerely.

'Don't worry,' she motions to leave. 'In the unlikely event you ever meet them, I'll be sure to let you know,' she says, her voice lightening.

'I'm not going to give up,' I vow.

She turns back with a smile and a twinkle in her eye and answers, 'I'm an angel, remember and as far as I can tell you're a mere mortal... I don't think it would work out very well!'

I call out after her. 'I'd still like to know what your criteria are.'

She ignores me.

As I watch her continue her rounds, I wonder if I really could be the man to meet them.

~Chapter 4~

5th September, 1944

It is a little time since that conversation, and after exercise, I ask if an orderly will push me out to a little courtyard so I can sit outside for a while.

Once on my own, I notice the vibrant flowers that adorn the flowerpots and cascade from the hanging baskets. With their fragrant smell, and the sunlight suddenly striking my face, I confess, it is a life-affirming moment, the first one in a long, long time.

Even the war is in its last throes; the Allies are taking all before them. Here in this small coastal town, there are fewer blackouts, and we have heard fewer air-raid sirens. Sitting here, it seems a world away.

After a while I identify fuchsias, honeysuckle and azaleas and many more, nature's splendour is all around me. I sit and spend a long time searching for the perfect flower with the perfect colour and the perfect fragrance. A fanciful notion I know...

Finally, I believe that I have found it. My light head is still spinning from this impromptu re-awakening.

I use my feet to help me navigate the wheelchair to the area. I can stand up, albeit unsteadily, then lean forward to collect my chosen specimen. Unfortunately, just as I try to sit back down, the wheelchair flips over. I collapse into a heap onto the hard stone ground.

Suddenly, I hear a shout from a hospital porter who comes rushing to my aid. I am promptly brushed down, and he helps to ease me back into the chair; ironically, he frets about a few scratches and a tiny amount of my spilt blood.

I am soon bandaged up by Nurse Gibbs and sent back to my ward.

Later, Nurse Brooks stops by my bed and places her hands on her hips, half scolding, half amused. Guiltily, and with eyes down, I am like a schoolboy caught apple scrumping or something.

'I hear you've been getting into trouble again.'

'I just wanted to smell a flower.'

'Really. I hope it was worth it,' she says, glancing at my bloodied knuckles, her face full of sympathy.

'It was worth it,' I assure her. I open the palm of my hand to reveal a perfectly symmetrical flower in a most delicate shade of aqua blue.

Her eyes light up as she holds it in her own hand. 'I have to admit, it is beautiful.'

'It's for you.'

Slightly taken aback, she takes the offering.

'Fancy that!' she laughs. 'Thanks,' she says, 'thanks ever so.'

Suddenly, her demeanour softens and I can see a tear in her eye. She turns and wipes it away.

I am not sure exactly what she is thinking, but I think it touches her momentarily, a small kindness, maybe, against a backdrop of so much suffering and pain.

Nurse Brooks looks to the ceiling and holds back the tears. She utters, 'This is so difficult...'

'Why is it difficult?' I ask quietly.

She does not reply, but holds me in an embrace for a few moments. For the first time, she seems oblivious as to what Matron might say or do.

She begins to cry onto my shoulder. 'This war...' she mutters. 'I wish it was over and everything was back as it used to be.'

After a while, she regains her composure.

'Jack,' she says in a gentle voice. 'This might not work out how you or I want it to.'

I view her misty eyes. 'Why not?'

She pauses and seems to choose her words carefully.

'Our situation, our relationship, is a simple suspension of reality. Your feelings aren't real; they are magnified because I'm taking care of you. I'm your nurse, that's all, and I could lose my job if Matron realised. Besides, you will be gone in a few weeks.'

'Where to?' I ask in surprise.

'Oh, a rehabilitation facility, I suppose. They'll set it all up for you, and when you do go, you will probably forget about me.'

'I'm quite sure I won't. My feelings aren't a suspension of reality or magnified in any way. They're real - bloody real!'

'Trust me; you have to find your past.'

'Why?'

'Please.' Nurse Brooks shakes her head and glances at the flower. 'Forget-me-not.' She pauses and raises her eyes. 'How could I ever do that?'

Nurse Brooks surreptitiously glances up and down the ward, leans over, and gives me a light kiss on the right cheek.

'Was that a goodbye?' I ask.

'Not quite yet.'

'So, what was the kiss for then?'

'For being you and for the flower, of course.'

'I'll pick a hundred flowers tomorrow,' I promise.

'Don't get any ideas from that.' She laughs as she brushes away a tear from her eye. 'But thanks for the thought, anyway.' She walks away with the flower held close to her chest.

~Chapter 5~

12th September, 1944

It is a week later and Nurse Brooks walks hesitantly into my temporarily ordained room.

'What are you doing back in here?' she whispers and shakes her head slowly back and forth. 'You promised me...'

She sits down and studies me intently. 'I thought you were doing so well with me.' She gives a sad smile and stares unerringly at me.

'Anyway, I have something to cheer you up,' she says after a while, with a sudden glint in her eye.

She quickly leaves the room and I watch the blur of her shapely stockinged legs as she goes. She returns a few moments later with a haversack; it is khaki, of medium-size, and slightly washed out. As if in triumph, she suddenly pitches the bag onto the bed.

I glance across to the incoming object, and even in my weak state, the mystery bag gains my attention.

Nurse Brooks pulls up a chair and sits down with a flourish. She moves in close in order to talk. I notice she is breathing more heavily than normal. I can only guess the reason for this is a mixture of her haste in seeing me, and some unknown excitement.

'What's this?' I ask.

Her brown eyes light up. 'Your belongings!'

'This bag really belongs to me?' I query, giving it the once over. 'There's no name or even a unit number on here.'

'Nurse Grant told me they left it here for you this morning. They assured her it was yours.'

My eyes flicker with uncertainty, and I shrug. 'I suppose it must be, then.'

She props me up as if I am going to watch a show of some sort. I follow her enthusiastic cue.

'Go ahead, Jack.'

Jack... When I first regained consciousness, I was told that my name was Jack, and that I had muttered it in my sleep.

I hesitantly run my index finger along the outside of the bag and then stop when I reach the clasp.

'Go on then,' Nurse Brooks urges. 'No time like the present.'

I pause and fleetingly wonder what secrets the contents might reveal about me. I remove my hand altogether.

'What is it?' she asks impatiently.

'It's jammed and won't open.'

Her excitement disappears like a deflating balloon. She rolls her lips as she confirms my initial observation.

'Perhaps I can force it open,' she says.

I give a hollow chuckle at the offer.

She takes out a little penknife of sorts from her pocket, one much like a Swiss army style, then glances back to me as if she can read my thoughts.

She stands up. 'My job covers a lot of things.'

'Does it?'

She fails to acknowledge me, and she flicks through several devices before settling on something resembling a tin opener.

I lean my chin on my fist and study her unguarded. Her oval face is clean and her skin is fresh, her almond-shaped eyes are framed by slender eyebrows and delicate eyelashes. Her honey-sweet lips are full and eminently kissable...

When I have nearly forgotten about the bag altogether, she looks over and tries not to smile.

'Can you at least show some interest? This might throw some light on who you are.'

'Sorry, I was distracted by the perfume you are wearing - it's lovely.'

Nurse Brooks returns an accepting sort of smile.

'If it really is mine, then let me,' I insist, catching her not-so-subtle drift. She pauses and relents. 'Okay, go ahead.'

I take the knife in my 'wrong' hand, or rather my left hand, and make a pathetic stabbing motion towards the clasp. Once again, I stab at it, as if opening a bottle of beer and miss altogether. I have no coordination or strength and quickly admit defeat. I chuck the knife across the bed and bite my lip like a spoilt child.

The nurse shows no irritation at my crass behaviour. Strangely, I notice her eyes are now moist.

I glance towards the stub of my missing arm.

There is no hand beyond my loose pyjama sleeve, there is no arm either, just my stub hidden away like a guilty secret. I presume my right hand and arm were left on the battlefield.

I stick out my chin. 'Go ahead then.'

'Are you sure you are ready to do this?' she asks.

I croak like a frog in agreement before my voice recovers to its recent whisper. 'I really am as curious as you are. Possibly, if I'm honest...' I peek into her eyes, '...a little scared even.'

'Scared of this? After what you've been through?'

I nod slowly. 'Of whom I might be. Suppose it turns out I'm not a particularly nice person?'

She laughs at the apparent absurdity and pauses, playfully considering the alternative.

She shakes her head and a strand of her long hair comes loose from her cap.

'In fact, I can tell you're all right,' she assures me.

'Am I?'

Her smile is utterly disarming, and she gently brushes the hair back from my forehead.

I can't help wondering if she does this as a woman or as a nurse.

'You're quite alright, actually.'

'How can you tell?'

She tilts her head slightly, as if in thought.

'I think it must be your blue eyes,' she says, half-serious and half-teasing.

'Really.'

'They are windows to the soul. Aren't they?'

'So, what do you see?'

She briefly glances behind her, turns back and says, 'Well, let me take a look now.'

She leans forward, her face just above mine, and playfully appears to 'lose herself in my soul', by producing a vaguely ridiculous and rather amusing expression. (This involves simultaneously sucking in her cheeks like a fish and blinking her eyes).

I laugh spontaneously at her silliness. 'Can you see anything else in there?'

She straightens up and snorts. 'Perhaps a few murky dalliances, but everything else seems okay. Perhaps you are forming an overly emotional attachment to someone... don't worry, that will be cured in time.'

'I see.'

I glance at my missing limb. 'Mentally I might come to terms with my future, but I am not so sure about the past.'

Nurse Brooks squeezes my hand.

'I'll help you rediscover your past. I promise I'll be there for you. Don't worry.'

It's a start, but I'd prefer her to be there in my future.

~Chapter 6~

My confidante jams the tool into the clasp and, with a degree of violence, busts it right open.

'That should do the trick,' Nurse Brooks says.

It works, the mystery bag is open. I sit up, impressed. She smiles modestly and pushes the bag towards me. I lean forward further still, slowly open the flap, and my heart races as I hesitantly eye the contents.

As expected, there is the usual supply of rations, including boiled sweets, chocolate, jam, oatmeal, tea and tinned meat. There are the obligatory (standard issue) spare socks, flannel, toothbrush, paste, spare boot laces and a mug.

Nurse Brooks continues to take the lead. My eyes linger over a shaving kit, and I sense her gaze studying my expression as I inspect an army issue shaving brush, a tube of shaving soap, and a razor.

'Anything?' she asks, full of curiosity. 'Stir any memories?'

I smile wistfully. 'These are all generic.'

She pulls out the stub of a ticket from inside a billet of personal effects. 'This isn't generic.'

'What is it?'

'The ticket stub for a Gracie Fields show,' she says and carefully places this to one side as if it is of great value. 'Do you remember that? And whom you might have gone with?'

I couldn't.

Then a battered old watch is presented to me. I study the large dial and the worn leather strap.

'Do you recognise it?' she asks. 'Was it a gift from someone?'

I shake my head and Nurse Brooks, seemingly disappointed, slowly places it to one side. We repeat the process: this time it is a slim book, a collection of quotations. 'Maybe someone loaned it to you?'

I shake my head again. 'It's sweet of you to have tried,' I say. 'Besides, the most important thing is missing.'

'What's that?'

'My I.D. card. This could belong to anyone.'

Nurse Brooks nods and seems lost in thought.

'Hang on a jiffy,' I exclaim. I have managed to open a pocket on the outer section of the bag.

Surprised, I notice an old sepia photograph pushed inside. Nurse Brooks snatches it and seems taken aback.

'What is it?' I ask.

I notice that the colour in her face drains away before she passes the photograph over.

Upon examining it, I am quite taken aback. Featured is a very pretty woman; in fact, she looks like a model. She has dark hair, a slightly cheeky smile and sultry, generous lips – and she is all wrapped up in a W.A.A.F. uniform.

I immediately wonder if I had taken the photograph and elicited that smile of hers, and if so, what I might have said at that exact moment. I am just noticing the woman's shapely legs when Nurse Brooks interrupts.

'Do you remember her?' she asks in a quiet voice.

I shake my head. 'No.'

'She's very pretty,' she says, matter of fact.

I stare at the photograph, half-expecting something to twig in my mind, or recall a memory that I can build my past upon. I cannot. If I am unable to locate my past, how can I confront the future? I wonder.

The nurse rolls her lips, deep in thought.

'An old girlfriend perhaps?'

I am unable to confirm or deny this, an awkward moment passes as I strain my mind. Finally, the nurse takes the photo from my hand and studies it again.

'She appears as though she is in love...'

'The eyes?' I say, as I roll mine.

Nurse Brooks shakes her head and flips the photograph over for me to see. She stands there frozen.

'Is there some writing on the back?' I ask.

'There is a message,' she confirms and then, with difficulty, she reads it out loud.

'To Jack, my sweetheart. You are my love, my life for always. I love you.'

Nurse Brooks puckers her lips and makes three theatrical smooching sounds. 'That's three kisses.' She forces a smile. 'Seems like you've been unfaithful.'

'How do you mean?'

'Giving another woman a flower...'

I reach for the photograph, study the writing and alternately turn from the image to the inscription and back again. I am dumbfounded.

'It means nothing. I can't even recall her or the message.'

'Not even the kisses?'

I roughly twist the yellowing edge of the photograph and grimace. My head, and I suppose my heart, hurts a bit as I try to recall this woman with whom I apparently share a past.

Worse still, this revelation compromises my budding relationship with Nurse Brooks. My disappointed expression is the cue for the nurse to gather up the contents and drop the bag onto the floor.

'Who knows,' I wonder, 'maybe I was once considered a bit of a charmer...'

Nurse Brooks smiles. 'Oh, there's no doubt you still are. You could charm the birds from the trees.'

'There is only one bird I really want to charm.'

'Well, you could.'

I turn away. 'Besides, those days are gone. Look at me now.'

'She'll want to see you, and if I were in her shoes, I would too.'

'Why?'

'Why not? Why are you so down on yourself?'

'Whatever we had, it's over. I don't think she'll want to see me, although it's irrelevant because I certainly can't remember her.'

'Come on, there will be plenty of time to recall. You need your rest.'

'I really don't remember her.'

'Not yet.' The nurse gives a wan smile. 'But she's out there waiting for you somewhere.'

'Why isn't she here then?'

'There's a war on. She's probably caught up in her work. Some soldiers have been away from their loved ones for years.'

I agree and try not to feel sorry for myself, but I still have no recollection, or any sentiment, towards the attractive young woman in the photograph.

That is when I notice that Nurse Brooks is downcast, miserable in fact.

'Are you sure you're all right?' I ask.

'Of course. It's this war. I have feelings too you know.'

I glance over to her, but she does not make eye contact. 'Of course you do, I'm sorry. I hate to see you upset like this. Is there anything I can do?'

We both notice Nurse Grant who has stopped in the doorway and views the bag and the photograph. She acknowledges Nurse Brooks with a curt nod, comes over and picks up the photograph.

'It seems like you have something to live for after all,' Nurse Grant says and smiles. 'That's good.'

***

The next time I wake up, I am back in the main ward, the framed photograph of my 'model' girlfriend is on my bedside table and Nurse Brooks is busy in another ward altogether.

~Chapter 7~

Here's what I know (from what I have been told).

I have suffered severe injury and trauma from mortar shelling during the invasion of Normandy on D-Day.

I have no memory and my arm has been blown right off, but I am alive. Many of my comrades were less lucky; they have been killed or have numerous missing limbs.

The discharge officer has told me how lucky I am, (any closer and the exploding shell would have been over my head). Luck comes in degrees or in my case - feet - I have learned.

Doctor Berger has told me I have psychogenic amnesia, which is a consequence of my shell-shock. After numerous scans and tests, he is confident that I do not have any apparent damage to the brain, my memories currently exist deep inside me, and the doctor is encouraged by this.

'They will return one day,' he promises. 'There will be a trigger; you might see something or someone who is familiar to you. If this happens, it could prompt your memory return. I'm quite sure of it.'

I am less sure though. The photograph from my haversack has not brought back any recollections, not yet at least.

Doctor Berger says, 'You have everything to live for,' and the nurses concur.

'Chin up' and 'You'll be right as rain', they all say, again and again.

It is hard to have confidence in myself though. At this time, I do not even recognise my own name. Everything I know is what I have been told. They call me 'Jack' (although there is no physical evidence that Jack is my true name). Now, I am in a hospital in Bournemouth, in the south of England. The other stuff I have had to make up.

I still have the headaches. Sometimes it is if I am putting on memory-rendering glasses and I am starting to see, but then the memories are snatched away and my life is thrown back again into a blur.

'What's becoming of me?' I ask Nurse Brooks.

'All you can do is wait, your memory will return. The doctor said it will, it's just a question of time. I've seen it happen too.'

'And if it does, what do I do in the meantime?'

'You can make some new memories in your new home?'

I smile enthusiastically. This proposition warms my heart and sends a surge of light into my formerly dark mind.

For one wonderful moment the past has become irrelevant, it is the present that matters with the hint of something more in the future...

Later, the reality returns like a stab into my heart and the light is usurped from my head.

Nurse Brooks has not offered to make new memories with me. I watch as she leans over and squeezes the hand of a patient called Charlie in the next bed. Despondent and slightly embarrassed, I realise my angel has always been a nurse to me, a wonderful nurse, but no more and no less.

~Chapter 8~

27th September, 1944

Just before midnight, I am still awake. I hear some excited noises from outside and roll over to look out of the window. A number of soldiers are all about with their firearms at the ready. I watch them for some time.

Under the dim lighting, the soldiers re-group, and then head into the main entrance. I immediately know something is up. Numerous thoughts fly through my head regarding likely scenarios, most of them involving prisoner of war escapees that I have read about in the newspapers.

Everything goes silent for quite a while, and I presume that is that.

Half an hour later, I witness a man enter at the far end of the ward. He stands stock-still in the shadows, as if listening for his pursuers and calculating his next move.

A patient across from me notices him too, and we exchange a conspiratorial nod. The rest of the patients are neither awake nor aware of the impending drama.

With a great physical effort, I try to get out of bed as quietly as possible in order to investigate; the other patient must have the same idea, wanting to assist me with the man's potential capture too.

Before I have set a foot on the floor, the intruder runs past my bed and into the nearby nurses' office, from where a scuffle ensues.

Two gunshots resonate like two claps of thunder before either of us can reach the office.

My heart sinks...and my head spins.... Who was in there? Please no... not Nurse Brooks...

Seconds later, I throw open the door. The man, in his final moments of life, slumps next to an already prostrate nurse. We push him aside in order to resuscitate the poor woman.

Chaotic scenes follow: lights go on, patients wake up and directions are hollered from the incoming soldiers, who are followed by doctors and nursing staff.

Shaken, we are pushed aside as the medical staff intervene. We stand back and wait in hopes of a miracle.

Then, we watch in horror as they take away two lifeless bodies. Slowly they all leave, except for an officer who stops and asks me some questions for his report.

Afterwards, a number of us, including nurses, sit about not saying much, neither wanting to go to sleep nor to be awake. When we recall our personal memories of the deceased nurse, it brings tears to our eyes. Someone makes some hot tea and we sit and talk some more.

Sitting on the edge of my bed, I reflect upon the death and destruction I have witnessed during my involvement in the war; tonight's incident has hit me the hardest of all. I am angry too, frustrated that the intruder hadn't chosen to fight against me, or against any one of us. It is such a cowardly act.

I learn later that the intruder was a local man of German extraction. His real name was Erich Muller, (locally, he had gone by the name of 'Eric Miller') who had been operating as a German spy. He had been sourcing military secrets by various methods, sometimes simply by visiting social establishments frequented by military personnel. His radio signals from a Bournemouth bedsit had been intercepted and he was forced to flee.

Secrets were gratefully stolen and then filtered: Britain's coastal defences, deployment of troops, civilian and troop morale and possible invasion targets and schedules.

If caught earlier, he might have been useful to the Security Service. Possibly he could have been 'turned' to become a double agent.

A campaign of misinformation had saved countless lives in Operation Fortitude during D-Day.

The idea was to plant bogus information, using numerous double agents to fool the Germans into thinking the invasion was coming at a place it was not, and that it was not coming to the place that it actually was.

I assume that once backed into a corner and on the run, he was seeking a temporary place to hide when he stumbled upon the hospital, our ward and then encountered the on-duty nurse. Emboldened, she had fought back when he had forced her to remain silent.

Sadly, in the struggle that followed, he took Nurse Gibbs' life. She was 28 years old, a wife and a mother. There seems to be little meaning to the killing, another senseless waste of life in the onslaught of war. This time it has happened in a hospital, to a nurse who was trying to help save lives.

As soldiers we accept our fate on the drawn lines of the battlefield. This, however, seems to be particularly cruel because it involves one of our beloved nurses. I reflect upon the number of innocent casualties, the ones that were seemingly forgotten. There are no medals for them.

Words are unable to express the terrible sadness which prevails across both staff and patients. Depressingly, this is to be one of my last nights at St Stephen's Hospital.

~Chapter 9~

30th October, 1944

I have spent over four months in hospital before being discharged and sent to a military rehabilitation shelter for disabled soldiers.

Contrary to Dr Berger's promise, I am still unable to remember anything about my past. The time before my service to my country is a complete and utter blank.

The pretty woman in the photograph did not show up, and the only time I think of my past is when I glance at that old haversack, now stashed away in a corner.

It is only natural for me to wonder, and I have pulled it open, and lost myself in thought. My present reality always returns to overwhelm any thoughts of my past.

I lie here on my own, living half a life and wonder where I should be and what I should be doing, and with whom. My sleeping pattern has been the same. I turn restlessly each night; sometimes I get up, take some tablets and fall back to sleep; other times I lie awake, while my random thoughts drift in a heavy and unsettled way.

My new home is called Bear Cross House. It seems an apt name as there are a few living here with crosses to bear.

It is a hastily converted Victorian school house divided into a dozen or so rooms. It is not luxurious by any account, but basic and comfortable. A small, neglected playground outside functions as a patio for the men.

Inside it is damp and dull and the fittings are cheap and cheerful but, after the hardships of war, it is adequate enough.

After I arrive at the shelter, I run into a neighbour, or to be exact, he runs into me. On the second evening, he knocks on my door. I give him the once over: he is as thin as a rake, has a wispy moustache and wears a tan army beret.

I soon discover my fellow resident is rather forward, which some might find irritating, yet quite disarming and I have to say he has a peculiar charm which compels me to like him.

'Harry Barnes,' he introduces himself. 'Just been demobbed.'

'Jack.'

'Settling in all right?'

'Fine thanks,' I mutter.

'What's the reason you're here?' he asks.

'Well, my arm...'

'It's a leg for me,' he interrupts, pulling up his corduroy trouser leg and exposing his artificial limb right there in the hallway. 'Where did you lose yours?'

'Normandy.'

'North Africa.' He smiles wistfully.

'I lost my hair too,' he says excitedly and whips his beret off. 'It just fell out one day.'

I soon realise that, absurdly, Harry seems to be enjoying this mutual sharing of physical losses.

'I think I may have lost a tooth...' I offer, rolling my tongue around my mouth.

'Half my ear's gone,' Harry says, 'see.'

I take a look; he is right, it is half-gone.

'I'm slightly deaf in my right ear,' I share.

'My toe has been amputated,' Harry says. 'I can't blame that one on Jerry though.'

'I've lost my memory.'

Harry rubs his chin in disbelief and returns a blank stare. 'Well, you got me, I can't beat that.'

'It's just temporary,' I assure him.

'They told you that?'

'Yes.'

'Huh.' He goes silent for a moment. 'Which regiment?'

I shake my head. 'I'm not really sure.'

'You really don't remember anything at all?'

'Nothing before I...'

'...Lost your arm, old man?'

I nod.

'Blimey,' Harry says, 'there are a few things I would like to forget.'

I mutter solemnly, 'Yes, I know the war...'

'No,' he snorts. 'A few women!'

'Oh, I see.'

'You got a girl?' he asks.

'There is someone.'

'I'm not surprised. Getting married next I expect.'

'No, it's complicated.'

'Ah, one of those!' He laughs. 'I stay away from that kind.'

I shrug. 'Maybe you're right.'

'I'm always right about affairs of the heart. It's one of my areas of expertise.'

He laughs again and pats his pockets, searching for something. 'Say, do you have any coffin nails, old man?'

I take out a packet of cigarettes and offer him one.

Harry reciprocates and pulls out a box of matches. Soon we are blowing smoke together.

'So, your memory really has gone completely.' Harry exhales. 'That's a rum deal.'

'Not at all. There's worse off than me.'

'Say, do you want to drown your sorrows? Or raise your spirits?'

I chuckle and query, 'Half-empty or half-full glass sort of thing?'

'Whichever you prefer.'

'I'm more a half-empty glass at the moment.'

'No problem.'

'What have you got?' I ask.

'A bottle of red ink, some pre-war beer, some aged whisky, and some dusty bottles of liqueurs pushed back in a cupboard somewhere.'

'Tempting.'

'You do remember how to drink don't you?'

'I'm more concerned about *what* I'm drinking.' I laugh. 'Besides, some things you don't forget.'

'I can see you'll fit in just fine here,' he says, 'You have a cracking neighbour too.'

'Who's that?' I ask.

'Me!' He laughs. 'I should warn you the walls are paper thin. The last fellow snored like a trooper. You don't snore, do you?'

'No,' I lie.

'Good. I'll be able to get a good night's kip then.'

Right on cue, I hear a cough from the other side of the wall.

'Who lives on the other side of me?' I ask.

'Oh, that's Peterson, Royal Artillery, but he's a dry, old stick.'

'I see.'

'Nice to meet you, Jack.' He thrusts his hand out. 'I can see you're a good 'un.'

He shakes my hand up and down with great enthusiasm. 'Come on then, I can help you try to remember, and you can help me try to forget.'

I smile as I reclaim my hand. 'It's a deal.'

I go to Harry's room and the evening turns out to be far from dull. He locates that bottle of red wine (or 'red ink' as Harry calls it), wipes the dust off those bottles of liqueurs and we drink all the beers. After a few hours, when I have finished sampling his whisky, I unwittingly thank my host (who has already passed out in his chair).

I observe Harry slumped there, his beret still on his head but set skew-whiff. I stagger over and clumsily straighten it for him; he doesn't open his eyes but mumbles as if saying his last, dying words, 'Thanks old man... we'll have to do this again sometime.'

I wish Harry a good night.

Upon leaving Harry's room, in spite of my new abode being just next-door, I turn the wrong way and go up the narrow hallway before turning back; my head is hazy, my legs are heavy, and the ceiling is spinning.

It takes a monumental effort to reach the comfort of my own bed. Strangely, when I do find it, I sleep soundly for the first time in many months.

~Chapter 10~

8th May, 1945

Bournemouth is still recovering from the conflict, and there is a special reason to celebrate the end of the war. The havoc caused upon this coastal town has been immeasurable.

On 23rd May, 1943, just two years ago, Bournemouth, like many other English towns and cities was the victim of a merciless air strike by German bombers.

With little warning, over 100 men, women and children were killed, and over 3000 buildings damaged. The air-raid sirens had sounded over eight hundred times previously but this was the most devastating attack on the town, hitting such landmarks as the Metropole Hotel and the Central Hotel. The 26 Focke-Wulf 190s dropped 25 high-explosive bombs in less than a minute. By the time the fighters were scrambled from R.A.F. base at Ibsley, all they could do was chase them out across the channel.

***

From my barstool at the Three Crowns Public House, I overhear the sing-song revelry from the street. A brass band starts up, signalling the end of the war celebrations, although my small part in the war has been over a long time.

Inside, under the Union Jack bunting, the patrons sing to the accompaniment of a piano. The smell of spilt beer, tobacco and the vinegar from fish and chips pervades the lounge with its uneven floor, low ceilings and beams.

Soon, some are drunk from the alcohol and some are simply drunk from the recent news; it reminds me of New Year's Eve. I sway to 'Roll out the barrel' in an attempt to join in, but I am sober in both senses.

Of course, I am happy the bloodshed is over, the Allies have won and Hitler is defeated, and the patrons have reason to celebrate, having reclaimed their daily lives and their way of life.

I have nothing to return to, nothing to reclaim, and even the drink cannot make me forget because I have nothing to forget. My emotions fluctuate because I am so alone, yet I am at the biggest party celebration in our nation's history.

I think of Nurse Brooks and a recent note she has sent me. She is 'thinking of me', she is excited the war has come to an end. She signs off with: 'Let's celebrate! But don't do anything I wouldn't do!'

I hear that Harry has been trying to locate me, but somehow, we have missed each other. He leaves a message saying he is going out early to celebrate. As yet, I haven't seen sight nor sound of him.

I have received a stream of pats on the back, hugs and handshakes, as everyone in a uniform has tonight.

From my barstool at the Red Lion (further up the road) I set up some beers for a few soldiers from the 1st Parachute Brigade who fought with great distinction in Arnhem.

They have been singing enthusiastically and torn off various numbers ever since I arrived. Standing next to me, they start up renditions of 'We'll meet again', 'Underneath the arches', 'Knees up mother Brown' and of course, 'Land of Hope and Glory' and 'Rule Britannia'.

Having made their not unsubstantial contribution, they move on. They had seemed keen for me to go with them, and I realise that some soldiers' sacrifices are more visible than others. They wrap their arms around my shoulders, and they whisk me away, consensual or not.

The kindred spirit of brothers in uniform envelops me and I burst into song which receives a great cheer. My audition must pass muster because I am matter-of-factly recruited to their casual ensemble.

I realise that I can recall the words to the songs I have heard and sung tonight, but it is deeply frustrating that, while I can do this, I cannot remember my own life... or even where or when I had sung these songs before.

From another barstool, this time at the Copper Kettle, I begin to relax and enjoy the party with my newfound singing friends.

I warm the seating and sample the ales at a few other locations, but each pub seems smokier, louder and fuller than the previous, so that we barely get through the front door to some establishments, let alone sit down. We push on through each time. The pattern is much the same.

'Go on!'
'Put your shoulder into it, we'll never get to the bar!'
'What's your poison?'
'Down the hatch!'
'Come on, another round!'
'Let's have another song!'
'One more for the road!'

With drinks in our hands, smokes and pipes never far away, we bellow out our songs. Soon twenty, thirty or forty patrons join in, and we nearly lift the rafters with the noise.

'Bless 'em all, bless 'em all, bless 'em all…' we sing.

The party carries on full-force. At one point, a colleague asks if I am all right. 'You look a bit peaky.'

'I'm fine,' I lie.

The toxic mix of alcohol, stale air and noise becomes too much for me, however, and I eventually pass out, collapsing onto the floor. My evening is over.

Miraculously, I somehow end up in my own bed. I presume that my friends have taken care of me. Their camaraderie is touching because they were not in any better shape than me, (they were decidedly the worse for wear in truth), but somehow, they have managed to carry me home.

And I guess they would have been singing all the way too, and with resilience like that, no wonder the Allies have won the war!

~Chapter 11~

20th May, 1945

Oh, yes. There's my angel, Nurse Brooks - or Lucy - as she finally shares in her recent letter.

You see, I haven't forgotten about her as she said I might, and we finally plan to go for that drink together.

Admittedly it was with a bit of prompting. I am nothing if not persistent, but the war has finished and as she says, 'A promise is a promise.'

She writes that she is going to spend the day with me and then stay with an old girlfriend in Southampton.

The day of our date is finally here. I shave, brush a dollop of brylcreme into my hair and put on my best lounge suit, together with a wide tie and a grey pullover underneath my jacket.

Putting on the tie is a bit of a problem, and in the end, I loudly knock several times on the adjoining wall to Harry. He pushes open my door as if answering to an urgent call for help. His eyes dart around the room as if following the flight of a fly, before his gaze settles on me.

'What is it?' he asks, breathless.

I point to my tie. 'I need some help.'

Harry sighs and crosses his arms. 'Your tie is the emergency?'

I nod and smile, trying to mask my inadequacy.

Harry smirks and comes straight over.

'What have we got going on here then?' Harry says, as he curiously inspects the tie wrapped haphazardly around my neck.

'It's the knot I can't do.'

'I suppose if I'd got here any later you might have strangled yourself,' he quips.

I scoff. 'Do you write all your own material?'

Harry flips up my collar and eyeballs me. 'So, tell me about this girl you're meeting?'

'She's beautiful,' I say. 'And sweet and smart.'

'So, what's she doing with you?' he jokes.

'Just concentrate on the tie, it has to be perfect.'

'Okay, okay.' He swats his hand. 'So, this girl, she's a nurse, isn't she?'

'That's right.'

'Say, does she have a friend?'

'No, and neither do I.'

'Ouch!' he says with a mock grimace. A moment later he pings the knot by flicking his finger. 'There you go old man, all done.'

I examine the shirt collar and tie in the mirror and smile in gratitude. 'Not bad.'

'I can see you really like this girl.' He looks me up and down and smiles. 'Is that why it's complicated?'

'In part.'

'Well, I'm off to do something uncomplicated.'

'What's that?'

'To eat and wet my whistle.'

I hardly listen as my thoughts are distracted at the prospect of my date with Lucy. I barely hear him say, 'I've replenished my drinks cabinet if you want to come over again, some time.'

Harry then jolts his head back as if receiving a cold flannel in the face. 'That was a good night!'

My eyes return to my tie; I call after him as he goes to leave. 'Oh, Harry...'

'Yes?'

'...You're a good sort, thanks.'

'What are friends for?' He gives me an exaggerated wink, makes a clucking sound and finishes with, 'Best of British.'

He has almost closed the door behind him when it opens again and he sticks his head back in; he points to the adjoining wall.

'You might want to have a code when knocking on that wall: one knock for emergencies, two knocks for anything else, know what I mean?'

'I do.' I nod.

'You see, it's not good for the old ticker.' He pats his chest. 'I don't want that on my ailments list too.'

***

Now Harry has gone, I gaze out of the window and catch a glimpse of a man across the road. He wears a scruffy raincoat and hat. When he sees me, he walks on.

I return and pick up my own hat: a fedora, and carry it in my hand; I stroll off in plenty of time to meet Lucy at our pre-arranged rendezvous, stopping off at a florist along the way.

~Chapter 12~

Earlier this morning it was still cool out, with the promise of sunshine. The sky is now the colour of lead; the sun is intermittent at best.

If that sunshine turns out to be a broken promise, I don't care, I am meeting Lucy. So, today, even rain would be a blessing!

I sit down at the Lyons Tea House in Bournemouth, pleasant enough, although nothing fancy either, lacking both linen tablecloths and ornate china, not that it would impress Lucy I sense.

I admit I have a few butterflies in my stomach; naturally I want the date to go well. On top of that, I have not seen Lucy for a while and I wonder if our conversation will be breezy or stilted.

I pick out a table with a good view and sit and wait. The longer I wait the more nervous I become.

I notice a button is loose and hanging by a single thread from my jacket. I fiddle with it idly, hoping it won't fall off. A contradiction I know. The button seems to take on greater significance as time goes by, and, absurdly, the success of my date (in my mind at least) becomes dependent on my button's thread staying intact.

There she is!

I go over and greet Lucy at the door with a hug and she gives me a kiss on each cheek. She is all smiles and apologies for being late, but she is here and that is all that matters.

And how good she looks!

Now dressed in her civvies, her curly hair flows free of her nurse's cap, her dress is looser not starched, and her shoes are fashionable not functional. She is a sight for sore eyes.

Once seated at the table, I present her with a single rose and she makes reference to the injuries I sustained from procuring my last offering.

'Did you have to smell the flowers again?' she jokes.

'Well, I did spend a long time in the florist's finding that particular one,' I admit.

The florist had been very patient and had seemed amused by my behaviour. I explained that I wanted a single bloom, and she watched as I went from flower to flower studying and smelling each one in turn.

Back and forth I went, up and down the shop and back again. After a while I asked her for her opinion. Quite possibly my enthusiasm was catching or alternatively, she just wanted to get rid of me, but as if on a mission, we were soon both sniffing away and looking for the 'perfect' specimen together.

Lucy admires the flower before smelling its scent. Then she gives me another kiss on the cheek. That is three; I am doing well.

We sit down, and she talks animatedly and at length, which is fine with me, because I don't have to worry about what to say.

I happily study her every expression and every mannerism. Some I recall from my time in the hospital, but some are new to me: the way she brushes her hair back behind one ear, the way she laughs, slightly self-consciously, the way she blushes if I am too forward. She laughs easily and often.

I am drawn to everything about her, from her rouge lipstick to her chocolate-coloured curls, to her charming smile that accentuates her soft cheekbones and to the wild spark hidden behind her eyes. I am entranced.

I compliment Lucy on her dress and its attractive shape which makes her smile.

'Oh, how I wish rationing was over!' she exclaims.

I blink. 'I thought it was.'

'Well, yes, for food of course...'

She is happy that rationing had ceased (for food), but she informs me that it is still in place regarding clothes.

'I didn't know,' I confess. 'But at least we can get a square meal now.'

She frowns. 'Men!'

'I suppose you would choose fashion over food?' I tease.

'Every time!' She laughs. 'Most of us girls would!'

I am happy to take an interest in fashion, her fashion. I size up her floral-pattern dress.

'Well, I think you look exquisite, beautiful.'

'Oh, this old dress...' she laughs. 'It's a utility dress.'

'It seems fashionable enough to my eyes.'

'Yes, but I want clothes with colour, style and panache - from Paris!'

'I'd certainly like to see that,' I say and give an empathetic sigh. 'I suppose you'll have to "make do and mend" a while longer.'

'Please don't remind me, anyway the war's over, I don't want to hear that slogan anymore.'

I nod. 'Well, you would still turn heads on a Paris catwalk.'

She laughs. 'I told you already, flattery will get you nowhere!'

'You can't blame a fellow for trying.' I shrug.

A while later, Lucy asks me, 'Did you enjoy VE day?'

I give a hollow laugh. 'Of course.'

She narrows her eyes. 'Anything else?'

'I confess...'

'This ought to be good!' she laughs. 'What do you confess to?'

'I suppose I was three sheets to the wind.'

'How do you mean?'

'Well, it's just that I can't remember how I got home.'

A smile stretches right across Lucy's face. 'You must have had a good time.'

A touch theatrically I rub my forehead. 'Judging from my headache the next day, I think I must have done.'

Lucy gives a knowing smile.

'What is it?' I ask.

'Oh nothing.'

I offer Lucy a cigarette and a light. 'A bribe for your secret thoughts.'

We share a smile.

'Well?' I ask after a moment.

'I don't give up secrets that easily.' She pushes her chin up and remains tight-lipped.

'Like that, is it?' I say.

'I'm afraid so.'

Then she breaks into a smile like that of a sun goddess and her cool eyes hypnotise me. The power of this simple act touches my empty heart, as though the sun has warmed me in the coldest of winters. I want to stay in this moment forever.

We share a comfortable silence as we smoke, and it is only broken when I smile. Lucy appears intrigued.

'Now you're the one with the secrets,' she says. 'What is it?'

'Oh, it's nothing really.'

'Oh, go on,' she urges gently, 'a penny for them.'

'It's just that I had a thought about this next-door neighbour of mine; he's called Harry.'

'What about him?'

'He wants me to ask you to invite some of your nurse friends over to the shelter.'

'Does he?' Lucy smiles. 'And what's this Harry like?'

'Relentless.' I smile, draw a puff and then blow the smoke over my shoulder. 'You know though...'

'What?'

'...Harry's become a friend, and he has helped me through some difficult times. Admittedly some of it has involved drinking large quantities of alcohol.' I laugh. 'But he's done it in such a way that I haven't even realised.'

'Well, good for Harry and good for you,' Lucy says. 'I'm really happy to hear that.'

'You should meet him some day,' I offer. 'It would be easy to arrange.'

Lucy is positive about meeting Harry.

'Are you happy there?' she asks. 'At Bear...?'

'Bear Cross House,' I confirm. 'I'm thrilled. Every time I walk around, I feel I'm back in detention at school.'

'It was converted from an old school?' she asks.

'That's what they tell me. Personally, I think it was from an old prison.'

'You make it sound so enticing; now I want to come and visit out of sheer curiosity.'

'Please do. You can always smuggle in a file, for our next escape effort.'

Lucy giggles. 'It can't be that bad.'

'Tell that to the tunnel diggers.'

***

Later, when we are eating our scones, Lucy studies me and I shrink, slightly self-conscious.

'Have you recalled anything else since I last spoke to you?' she asks.

'Yes,' I answer.

Her eyes dilate.

'What?' she asks, holding her teaspoon as if frozen in mid-air. 'What have you remembered?'

'I keep having flashbacks of a pretty young thing, an angel in fact, a nurse who works in a Bournemouth hospital.'

She returns the teaspoon to her saucer, then pulls out a compact from her handbag and reapplies her lipstick. 'Aside from me,' she clucks.

'Oh, then no.'

'I see,' she says and fidgets in a mixture of resignation and surprise.

'Why does the past matter?' I ask.

She glances up. 'If you don't know your past, how can you - or I - know who you really are?'

'The important thing is the present,' I say. 'You only have to look into my eyes to find me.'

'I know.' Lucy smiles, yet seems intrigued. 'But how about your heart?'

I smile. 'That's easy, that's where you'd find you.'

'Thank you.' Lucy flashes a smile and places her hand on mine. 'You haven't changed one bit, I see.'

'I am what you see, I suppose.'

Our eyes meet and, in that gentle, quiet way of hers, Lucy asks, 'What do you really want from life, Jack?'

I consider her question and answer it as truthfully as I can. 'Like most others I should imagine...' I pause.

Lucy gazes into my eyes waiting for my answer. I catch her nervously twisting the bracelet about her wrist.

'...To have someone to love, to care for and to grow old with.'

She breaks eye contact, lost in thought. 'I'm sure you'll find it.'

'What about you?' I ask.

'Much the same,' she says, her eyes welling up.

A split second later our waiter drops his tray of teacups at our feet. Our eyes meet and we laugh spontaneously.

'Is that a good omen?' I ask Lucy, after the waiter has made his profuse apologies to us.

'The power of a wish?' she smiles.

'Or two wishes?' I suggest, not being able to resist, but Lucy remains silent.

***

Later, when it comes to paying the bill, Lucy asks, 'Are we going Dutch?'

'No,' I say. 'My treat.'

In my haste to pay, I drop my wallet onto the floor. A shiny florin falls out and rolls over by her foot. She picks it up.

'See that: a perfect two bob bit.' She smiles as she turns the silver coin over. 'It might be worth something one day.'

'Yes, two bob probably.'

She goes to give it back.

'You keep it,' I offer.

'What for?'

'A rainy day.' I shrug. 'And you might want a cup of coffee.'

'Okay, I will.' Lucy tucks the coin into her purse.

When I extract the money in order to pay, I notice Lucy's expression is frozen and her eyes are glazed over.

'What is it?' I ask.

'They give injured soldiers artificial limbs you know,' she says after a while. 'It's quite common.'

I nod. 'Dr Berger had talked about arranging it.'

'You'd probably have to go to London for it: The Queen Mary Hospital. They have a wonderful programme, the best in the country.'

'I've read about it.' (I remember a news-story about the heroic Douglas Bader who received two prosthetic limbs and carried on flying in the R.A.F.).

'It will make your life so much easier,' she says. 'You should go. I'll come with you, if you like. Promise me you will go.'

I nod and make a promise.

Lucy tells me that since I have left the hospital, she now nurses soldiers coming out of the operating theatre: amputations, severe head and body wounds and even one or two like me. It has taken its toll on her.

After the refreshments, we step outside.

'Fancy a walk to the end of the pier?' I suggest.

'As long as you don't jump in,' she laughs.

'I won't,' I tease, 'if I don't have reason to.'

We head towards the re-opened pier and we are suddenly a happy couple enjoying an afternoon walk, temporarily free of the burdens of reality. The wind has picked up, and we brace ourselves by interlocking arms.

We are barely mid-way along, when the salt spray perforates the air and the wind comes suddenly in gusts.

We huddle together under an umbrella, take a seat, and view the seascape. The crying seagulls and the crashing waves provide the dramatic soundtrack.

Entranced by the power of the elements, we carry on in defiance, with Lucy's distinctive polka- dot umbrella as our only defence. The brolly is soon wind-shot and we share a laugh at the absurd-looking remains of this once fine piece of apparatus.

The rickety umbrella is now inversed, reversed, its metal ribs horribly exposed, and no longer attached to the ripped canopy; quite useless in fact.

A number of sightseers are coming the other way. 'It's getting pretty rough now,' one man comments as he walks past us. We take no notice.

At the very end of the wooden structure, we lean on the iron rails and watch as a fishing vessel pitches and rolls on the breaking waves, waiting for the incoming tide to take her home with her catch. My mind is in full flow although my thoughts are not about any fish.

As Lucy makes a move to walk back, my opportunity is slipping away. I grab her hand and pull her back towards me, in efforts to kiss her.

She playfully remonstrates and turns her flushed cheek to me.

'You are only on loan,' she teases.

'How do you mean?' I ask, still gripping onto her hand.

'You know what I mean.'

'Do I?'

'Your rightful owner will be along to claim you,' she laughs as she pulls away. 'I'm just taking care of you for now.'

I realise she is referring to that stupid photograph again.

'Why?'

'It's like a sisterhood fraternity,' she giggles. 'We stand by one another.'

'At the cost of your own happiness?'

She playfully pouts theatrically. 'We're very loyal.'

'Supposing she doesn't come?'

'I'm not a stand-in if that's what you mean.'

'I've never thought of you as one.'

'Look, imagine we court,' she says more seriously, 'and just as the doctor promised, your memories do return, then your girlfriend shows up - there'll be three of us, a love triangle. What a fine mess.' She throws her head back and then laughs aloud. 'No thanks!'

She skips off. I catch up with her and clasp her hand in mine again. I pull her towards me. Once again, she ducks and weaves.

'I will tell your dream girl,' she promises.

'Tell her what?'

'That you've been unfaithful.'

I use this as my cue. I lock my lips with Lucy's in a passionate kiss; she lingers before finally pulling away. She glances back in a mixture of shock and surprise.

'At least it's true now,' I say, 'the unfaithful bit.'

She nods in agreement. 'I suppose it is.'

We walk back without saying much. Finally, she turns to me and says, 'Jack - all we can ever be is friends.'

I hear her words but I don't really believe her for some reason.

'You will always be my friend, my best friend,' I say.

'Yes, I know, your angel,' she whispers.

The playfulness ends, Lucy becomes quiet and contemplative. She wishes me luck as she boards her train.

'Sorry about your umbrella,' I call out as the train begins to move off.

For my benefit, Lucy dangles the umbrella from the window and attempts to open it; of course, it is shot to pieces.

Then, she air-mouths a monologue and, although I do not have the faintest idea of what she is saying, she still continues. It is quite funny and very endearing. All I can do in response is to smile and shrug apologetically.

***

I do not try to arrange another date with Lucy. I know in my heart of hearts how she feels about me, and even wonder if there might be someone else in her life.

I suppose in truth, I have given up on Lucy and finally admit defeat.

~Chapter 13~

October 25th, 1945

Outside my window is a big old husk of a tree that stands distinctively on its own. I gaze out to this tree every morning, sometimes during the day and last thing at night. I'm not sure but I think it is a walnut tree.

In my fitful state, and perhaps weirdly, the tree is somehow watching over me, or perhaps it is because I have been looking at it too long. Whatever it is, I am drawn in by its presence. The only living organisms I see every single day are my neighbour Harry and the walnut tree. I don't know what that says about me, except to state that I don't get out too much.

It has been a while since I saw Lucy, five months to be exact. Autumn is dissolving into winter, the temperatures have dropped, the wind has picked up, and the sky seems permanently dark and rainy.

I haven't contacted her but of course I have thought about her. I'm certainly not expecting to see her.

It is a Saturday morning and I am sitting smoking my Woodbines. Through the window I gaze at my tree and watch the leaves swirl and dance in the wind.

Lucy suddenly enters the scene as if from nowhere. She strides across the leaves, collapses her brolly, then sees me and gives a wave.

I am not only surprised by her visit but in those few seconds I am alive again. I extinguish my cigarette and go to the door to greet her.

Remarkably, my angel is standing there before me, and smiling.

She pushes a coin into the palm of my hand.

'What's this for?' I ask, studying the florin.

She glances back over her shoulder. 'It's a rainy day - and I could do with a cup of coffee.'

'Well, I never!' I laugh and glance at my old coin. 'I only wish it had rained sooner.'

'Look at you,' she says a moment later, 'you've come on in leaps and bounds.'

'Have I?' I question.

'This place is just what the doctor ordered.'

'Dr Berger?'

She laughs. 'You know what I mean.'

Lucy breezes in and is full of initial chatter and charming bluster when she seems to run out of steam. She appears nervous as though something is weighing on her mind. I ask her if everything is all right, but it is as if she has put up a barrier and she simply returns a shrug.

As she surveys my books on a shelf in the sitting room, I ask, 'So, is there any special significance for your visit?'

'No,' she says and carries on perusing my collection of cheap Penguin paperbacks.

'No reason at all?'

She looks over. 'Oh well, I like to check up with my ex-patients.'

'Really?'

'Of course.'

'That must take up a lot of your time,' I smile.

'I like to keep in touch,' she says, not looking my way.

'But there must be scores of ex-patients you must still care about.'

She turns to me and says quietly, as if in confession, 'Actually, just you.'

I refrain from doing a jig of delight and kissing her. Instead, I simply listen.

'I suppose I was thinking about you one day, so I decided to come and see you.'

'I'm glad that you did. Is there anything I should read into this?' I ask, still curious.

'No, I just wanted to say hello, really.'

'So, you were thinking about me?'

'Yes,' she admits, 'as a friend.'

'I see.' I suppress a sigh and my expression gives away my true thoughts.

'I still care about you, you know,' she admits.

'Do you?'

'Of course, I do. You know I do. But...'

'As a friend.' I interrupt and nod, trying to be magnanimous. 'That means a lot to me and the care you gave me all those months,' I say quite truthfully. 'I'll never forget your kindness.'

The care Lucy has given me is above and beyond. Yes, she has nursed all of her patients, but she not only cares for me but, most importantly, she believed in me.

'You're welcome.' Lucy smiles. 'About this book...' she says, changing the subject and suddenly holding it under my nose. 'Is it any good?'

I read the title: August Folly by Angela Thirkell.

'Very good, quite amusing too, in a dry sort of way. You can borrow it if you like.'

'How would I be able to return it?'

'Just stop by whenever you've finished it.'

'Oh, that's okay.' She pushes the copy back and avoids eye contact. 'I can't commit to that,' she mutters. 'Oh, I mean I'm always so busy. I only get one day off a week.'

I look directly into her eye and indicate my missing arm. 'Is it about this?' I ask bluntly.

'Good heavens, no. That's irrelevant.'

'It doesn't seem like it to me some days - so how could it be for you?'

'It makes no difference at all.'

'Are you sure?'

'It's not about that,' she insists firmly. 'There's still so much going on.'

'I know, and on and blooming on - but I've missed seeing you.'

Lucy sighs. 'That's why I've come today. Like it or not, I have a job to do.'

'I'm sorry,' I say and let it go.

'But I see you didn't get to London?' she asks.

'Not yet.' I give a feeble smile. 'I will one of these days.'

She scoffs. 'And which day will that be?'

'How about a drink?' I ask, changing the subject.

'Do you have a G & T?'

'I'll be right back,' I say and head off to the kitchen.

Lucy sits down and stretches her legs out on the settee. 'Do you have any 78's?' she calls out.

'Records?' I ask. 'Of course.'

'Play something.'

'What?'

'Anything, as long as it's lively and fun.' She fluffs a cushion and props it behind her head.

'How about Glenn Miller?' I suggest.

'I love Glenn Miller.'

She kicks off her shoes. 'Do you mind?' she asks, and then leans her head back on a cushion before closing her eyes. 'I'm s-o-o tired.'

After her drink, exhausted, she drops off to sleep on my settee. I sit opposite, sip my beer and wait quietly until she wakes up.

An hour later, Lucy jolts, apologises and then smiles when I insist, I have enjoyed her (sedentary) company. We chat and the rest of her visit passes in a blur.

'You said you wanted to meet Harry?' I remind her. 'I'll give him a shout, shall I?'

'Okay.'

I knock twice on the wall. A few moments later Harry saunters in, as pleased as punch.

'What's cooking?' he says. 'Make it brief though, as I've got a lovely, young filly...'

'Harry,' I interrupt, 'I want you to meet Lucy.'

'Hello Harry,' Lucy says, stepping out from the shadows. 'Pleased to meet you.'

'Hallo!' His eyes widen. 'I say, in the daylight you're quite a beauty aren't you.'

'What a funny expression,' Lucy laughs nervously.

'Have you two met before?' I ask, quizzical.

'No, just a turn of speech, old man - meant as a compliment, you know.'

'Thank you, then.' Lucy is blushing now.

'Well, I say it as I see it.'

'Well, I can vouch for that,' I say to Lucy, 'he does.'

'Thank you for helping Jack, you know, with everything,' Lucy says.

'Oh, I try to help around here,' Harry smiles, 'I sometimes make the tea, chat to the inmates, that sort of thing, although,' he says with a wink, 'I've been known to throw a good bash too!'

'Yes, I heard.'

'Say, if you ever want to bring your nurse friends along, I could arrange a do. I'm sure the men here would be up for it.'

Lucy smiles at this. 'I'm sure. Perhaps I could bring my colleague, Nurse Grant too.'

Harry smiles awkwardly. 'Yes, of course, she would be welcome. The more the merrier.'

A moment after that, Harry makes his excuses and leaves.

We exchange doubtful glances because Harry is indeed a one-off.

After eating and before Lucy leaves, she helps me wash up. With one hand, I hold each dish in the soapy water while she washes it with a cloth. I then set it aside.

Standing so close, I can smell Lucy's perfume, see the hazel colour of her eyes, and hear her soft breath. Every so often we inadvertently brush against each other and I feel the softness of her hand. When we have finished, I turn to her.

'See that,' I say. 'We make a good team.'

'Yes, but look at that mess.' She indicates a pre-existing stack of dirty cups and plates on the counter. 'Don't you ever wash your dishes?' she scolds playfully.

'Only when I need them' I confess.

'You and your square meals I suppose.'

'Fashion over food, isn't it? And I must say you're looking rather lovely.'

'Flattery will get you nowhere.'

'You can't blame...'

'A fellow for trying,' she finishes. 'I don't.'

'Look at us, we're completing each other's sentences,' I say in surprise.

'Well, anyway, we're all done,' she says, straightening my tea towels. 'I best go.'

I try to help her on with her coat. Unfortunately, I make a right dog's dinner of it. All I can do is hold her jacket by its collar, but she is unable to thread either arm into the sleeves.

After several comic turns - which could have been out of an unscripted Laurel and Hardy routine - we double up in stitches.

After that I give up altogether. She has a twinkle in her eye. 'What am I going to do with you?'

A moment later, she turns to me and says, 'She'll find you, or you will remember where she is.'

I snort. 'Are you talking about that stupid picture again?'

'I'll expect an invitation to your wedding,' she follows up.

'I don't know the woman,' I say, and for seemingly the hundredth time. 'Besides, I can hardly marry a photograph.'

'You know her, you just don't know it yet,' she replies. 'Your memory will return anytime now. That's what the doctors assert.'

'Doctors! Can't they ever be wrong?'

'Never!' She laughs.

After that, our conversation subsides and I stand there in the hallway, staring at her. I am strangely tongue-tied and mute as if on a first date. The silence lasts for a few moments.

Various thoughts fly around my mind but it is finding the right thing to say. I briefly consider proposing to her but I know she will reject it outright. However, after having had that thought, anything else I might say will seem trivial.

'Cat got your tongue?' she asks and smiles sweetly.
'Well...' I say.
'Well...It was nice seeing you.'
'You too.'
'I suppose I'd better be off,' she says finally. 'I'm working first thing tomorrow.'

I see her to the door. Once on the doorstep she turns back, leans in, and kisses me on the cheek. I try to reach around her waist but she spins around like an elusive fish, wriggling away. Standing back from me she returns an impish smile.

'I know all your moves now,' she says and giggles before heading off.

'When will I see you again?' I call out.

'Close your eyes and you'll see me again,' she jokes.

'I love you,' I mutter under my breath, but of course Lucy does not hear me or turn around.

I watch as Lucy's slight figure recedes into the greyness and then she is gone. My heart sinks as the joy of seeing her evaporates, and my grim outlook is mirrored by those coming winter months. Suddenly my future seems pointless, in fact, black, as if I am mourning a death.

I trudge back in, sit down and stare out of the window again. I soon become lost in thought.

The twinge of regret concerns my missed opportunity. Might she have said yes to my proposal, I wonder. I am not quite as sure of her answer now...

Under different circumstances, I believe we might have built upon our rapport, the connection that we undoubtedly have. Unfortunately, it seems to be a forlorn hope.

My supposed 'dream girl' is in the way of any potential relationship between us. At least it is for Lucy. And so, in truth, I am finally compelled to find my past. Whatever it holds and whomever it might be with.

And, having made that decision I wonder if it might be the key to my remembering. Besides, I am left with no alternative.

~Part 2~

~Chapter 14~

October 30th, 1945.

With the worsening of the weather, I have been spending most of my time indoors, kicking my heels and twiddling my thumb. I am probably not good company to be around, to be honest. Even Harry has sensed my mood swings and has on occasion given me a wide berth.

One day, I happen to be out; there had been a break in the bad weather, and a little while after my return, Harry comes rushing into my room, excitedly. As usual, he is grinning away.

'I've been trying to find you.'

'What is it?' I ask.

'Someone came to see you today.'

He comes over, pulls up a chair, leans forward and sits inordinately close to me. Then he stares at me as if I'd just beaten his hand at Poker.

'Who was it?' I ask.

'I suspect it was someone from the military,' he says, scrutinising my reaction.

'Who was it?'

'That's the funny thing, he wouldn't say.'

'Was he in uniform?' I ask.

'No, though, he appeared connected.'

'Connected?'

'You know, an Oxford, boffin-type, spoke well, but he down-played it a bit. I think he'd slept in his raincoat; he was a crumpled mess to be honest.'

'Did he leave a message?'

'No, he said he might return some other time.'

'What did he say?'

'Just that they had heard that you might be here, and that they were missing one of their own.'

'One of their own?'

Harry shrugs. 'I asked him that, but he wasn't telling.'

'He asked for me by name?'

'Not exactly, he asked to speak to the occupier of this room.'

'Anything else?'

'No, I said that you had lost your memory.'

'What was his response?'

'That he shouldn't bother you and it's best to leave the past in the past, or something like that.' Harry catches my eye. 'Are you sure you weren't working for Special Ops?'

Now I was the one to shrug. 'I presume I was just a raw recruit and a private in the army.'

'And that's all?' Harry asks. He seems to be considering me differently now: out of the side of his eyes. I realise what Harry is intimating.

'You don't honestly think that I am using my memory loss as a ruse to cover up some nefarious deeds I might have done as an agent of some sort?'

'Well, maybe you are,' Harry says furtively, 'and maybe you aren't.'

'Harry!' I bark. 'Please!'

'Okay.' Harry smiles. 'I believe you.'

'Which bit?'

'I believe you can't remember - but you still might have been involved in some spying, and a bit of treachery!'

'You do have a suspicious mind,' I reply.

Harry wanders off again and mutters, 'It's always the quiet ones...'

I mock Harry and playfully throw my slipper (the first thing that comes to hand) towards him and the door.

But now alone, secretly, I consider the possibility that he could be right.

Since then, whenever I peer out from my window, I'm on the look out for someone who fits Harry's description of 'a crumpled mess' and who might be an 'Oxford, boffin-type'. No luck yet.

***

For the umpteenth time, I pull the haversack from a far corner of my room. There is something about that photograph that I may have previously noticed but it hasn't consciously registered. That must be the only reason I can think of, as to why I have an irresistible urge to re-examine it.

I place the photograph flat under a bright lamp. When I ignore the pretty female W.A.A.F. in the foreground and examine the background, I notice there is a sign, a fixture of some sort on the ground.

It is undoubtedly very small, and the lettering is not readable, at least not to the naked eye.

I quickly realise that the sign is probably that of the name of an air base, in fact, a big clue to the location of where the picture has been taken.

I crash my fist hard against the wall. Harry, as ever, comes dashing into my room.

'Do you have a magnifying glass?' I ask him.

'I was just trying to catch forty winks,' Harry says and gives off a disaffected expression. 'You expect me to believe that this is an emergency?'

'Look at this.' I go to show him the photograph.

'H-e-l-l-o! Who's this?' he asks, immediately gravitating towards the picture. 'I'll get the magnifying glass, shall I?'

In the meantime, I pull up a chair and sit at my desk. A moment later Harry returns, his forty winks long since forgotten.

'What do you know about this beautiful creature?' he asks, peering over my shoulder.

'Nothing at all.'

'May I?' I ask, as I take the magnifying glass from Harry's wandering hand.

'Hey! Can I have a gander too?' he asks after a moment.

I scoff and click my tongue. 'I'm not interested in her; I'm looking at this sign.'

'Oh,' he mutters and then squints.

'What sign?'

'I know where this was taken,' I say as I scribble the name on a piece of paper.

'Where?' Harry asks in surprise.

I push the paper under his nose.

'R.A.F. Hawkinge?' he queries.

'In Kent,' I confirm. 'I think I have a chance of finding her.'

Harry enthusiastically takes his turn with the magnifying glass. 'How on earth could you have forgotten her?' Harry says. 'It doesn't seem possible.'

I shrug.

'Well,' he says, 'this is one it would seem worthwhile re-acquainting yourself with.'

~*Chapter 15*~

October 31st, 1945

I take a train and then a bus to Woodchurch in Hampshire, to see the pretty woman in my photograph. Upon arrival I get off the bus, walk past some garden allotments and then on by the parish church.

Near to an 'olde' public house is a row of thatched roofs that sit atop lime-washed stone cottages which gleam brightly in the morning sunlight.

Out of sorts and slightly out of place, I watch villagers going about their business. An elderly man with secateurs is busy snipping away at a privet hedge; the postman delivers hand-written letters; a woman props her bicycle outside the post office and visitors return laden with second-hand books and all manner of bric-à-brac from the church jumble sale.

I observe two dogs play chase on the village green; out of sight, from under one of the garden seats, a wise, old cat lazily opens half an eye at their activity.

Running parallel and close to the cottages is a gentle stream with man-made crossing-points, little more than stepping stones which are placed at regular intervals. I cross one of these little arched bridges.

Nervously, I draw and release the knocker of one of the stone cottages. I step back from the squat, oak door and wait; a moment later, I knock again.

Is my past about to appear before me?

After a while, a young woman appears wearing stained dungarees and green wellington boots, holding a bunch of sweet alyssum in one hand.

'Sorry, I was out the back, doing a bit of gardening. I wasn't sure if it was a knock or not.'

A dog, a spaniel I realise, comes excitedly up by the owner's side, its tail wagging and its eyes inquisitive.

'Sit Chester,' she orders.

And, in a flash, the dog sits down. I bend to rub Chester's ears and mutter, 'Such a good dog.'

I straighten up and push the photograph back into my wallet. The woman at the door appears to be the same person pictured, albeit she is more casually attired. She has the same hourglass figure, the same smile and even her hairstyle is unchanged.

'So, how can I help you?' the woman asks, quizzical, giving me the once over.

'I really hope you can.'

I am taken aback by her failure to recognise me, and immediately draw two possible conclusions: she thinks it is indelicate of me to show up at her front door if she is in another, new relationship (her manner is a little taciturn), or she doesn't know me at all. I plough on anyway.

'Yes?' she asks.

'I'd like to talk to you.'

'What about?' she queries.

'About me... and possibly you.' (The conversation is mightily awkward). 'Do you remember me?' I ask, shifting my feet.

The woman's eyes lift in thought. 'What's your name?'

'Jack.'

'I'm not sure what you want or what this is about.'

'It's about the fact that I am still alive. You see, I believe that it is my duty to let you know.'

The woman eyes me with great curiosity.

'Thank you?' she says in a mixture of amusement and puzzlement.

'Oh, of course,' I say. 'I understand if you might have given up on me, or moved on. You know, the war - it's completely understandable.'

I peek through into the hallway. 'I promise I will be discreet,' I whisper. 'This won't take a second.'

The woman looks back, too. 'I'm still not entirely sure I know what you're talking about.'

'I have a photograph to show you. Can I come in for a moment and explain?'

She looks me over, sees my missing arm and has taken pity on me.

'I was in Normandy,' I say. 'I've lost my memory as well.'

She gives me a sad, empathetic smile, one that should be reserved for funerals or receiving particularly bad news. I am fine, really.

'Okay, sure,' she agrees. 'Come on in.'

I follow my curvaceous hostess and Chester into the hallway and then to the sitting room.

'This is charming,' I say, and then take a moment to survey the cottage's interior.

The sun streams through the little lead-glass windows. Set upon various sills and tables are fresh flowers in vases.

Elsewhere, books and brass ornaments adorn the shelves and in centre place, a fireplace, framed with decorative tile and an iron hearth set below.

When I raise my eyes, I notice a barometer on the wall, and here and there are various country landscape scenes all in watercolours and set in decorative gold frames.

In a corner stands an old-fashioned writing desk with pastel notecards and coloured envelopes that are pushed into the cubby holes of the desk. A blotter is situated next to a small bottle of ink and a pen.

I immediately imagine her sitting and penning her personal letters on floral designed stationary as Chester sits dutifully by her side; notes to herself, and cards to her friends and family.

Has she has ever written something to me...I wonder.

'Have a seat,' my host offers. I sit down and begin to babble nervously.

'Just to say, first off, we're just friends, Lucy and me, nothing more - at the moment - she always encouraged me to try to find you.'

'Who's Lucy?'

'Well, where to start?' I ask rhetorically. 'She's an angel really. I first met Lucy at St Stephens, when she was working as a nurse...'

I carry on in much the same vein for a couple of minutes or more before she interrupts.

'You said there was a photograph?'

I take the photograph from my wallet.

The woman places the flowers to one side, takes the picture and studies it.

'That is you, isn't it?' I ask after a moment.

'Yes, of course,' she smiles. 'I remember it being taken.'

'Did I take it?'

The woman is silent, forlorn. 'Where did you get this?' she asks.

'I found it in my belongings.'

'Your belongings?'

'Yes,' I whisper.

The woman slowly shakes her head and then shrugs.

'You mean you weren't my fiancée or my girlfriend?' I ask.

'No. Why would you think that I was?'

'Look, like I say, I will be discreet if you are married now.'

'I'm not married.'

'Or engaged?' I prompt.

'I'm not engaged either.'

'So, you didn't know me a year or more ago.'

'No, not then - not ever.'

'And this message you wrote on the back - that wasn't directed to me?'

She flips it over, and studies it closely, slowly reading the words. She raised her head. 'I didn't write this.'

I place my hand on my temples in a mixture of confusion and frustration.

'I still don't understand how you got my picture,' she says.

'Like I said: it was in my bag.'

'Listen, I don't wish to be rude, but who are you?'

'I'm Jack,' I repeat.

'But I still don't understand; I've never seen you before in my life.'

'Then I don't understand either,' I say, frustrated. 'I'm sorry about this. I feel a bit of a fool coming here now.'

I get up to leave.

'Sit down – please.' The woman gives a semi-smile in sympathy. 'How were you to know if you've lost your memory?'

'That's the whole problem.'

'Listen, I've been working in the garden all morning. I'm parched,' she says. 'How about a cup of tea or something stronger?'

'Tea will be fine,' I smile. 'That would be good of you. Thank you.'

'I'm Phyllis by the way.'

'I'm Jack.'

She smiles wistfully. 'Yes, I've figured that bit out.'

She goes away to prepare the tea. In the meantime, I notice that Chester hasn't moved. He just sits a few feet away, all the while, staring at me.

Phyllis returns a short while later with a tray set with two cups and saucers and a teapot. She puts it down and glances over to Chester, still obediently sitting there.

'Has he been good?' she asks.

'Surprisingly good.'

She sits down and pours. 'Right,' she says, 'can we start at the very beginning?'

'Of course.'

'How did you find me?'

I tap my finger at the air base sign, the one set out in the distance.

'You could see that?'

'With a magnifying glass, yes, I could. I visited R.A.F Hawkinge, and they were able to help locate you to here in Woodchurch.'

'What about your memory?'

'Bits of it come back from time to time, snippets here and there.'

'But you do know your own name?'

'Yes, but someone even had to tell me that.'

'What of the mystery of my photograph ending up in your belongings?'

I roll my shoulders.

'I hope so, but it still seems strange. Why would anyone write on the back of it?'

I shook my head. 'I know a few places I can make an enquiry about it.'

'It doesn't make any sense.'

'So, who did take the photograph of you?' I ask.

Phyllis glances away and then says, 'My fiancée.'

'But I thought you said...'

'He was killed in the war.'

'Oh, I see.'

'He was a pilot in the R.A.F.'

'I'm so sorry.' A moment of silence passes before I add, 'He must have been a true hero.'

'Thank you. I think he was; they all were.'

The pieces are coming together, although I am not sure how the photograph has arrived on my doorstep.

We talk some more over tea. An hour at least has passed, and realising I am impressing upon her time, I thank my hostess for her help.

'Can I keep this photograph of you?' I ask.

She eyes me oddly.

'For my friend, unless of course it is inappropriate...'

She interrupts, 'Why does he want it?'

'I think he has taken a shine to you.'

'To stick on his wall?' She laughs.

'Probably.'

'What's his name?'

'Harry Barnes.'

Phyllis smiles shyly. 'That will be all right I suppose.'

As we part, Phyllis gives a wry smile and then remarks insightfully, 'It seems like you haven't given up on your Lucy, have you?'

'You're right, I haven't' I smile back. 'I was duty-bound to see you. Lucy calls it her sisterhood fraternity.'

'I see.'

'With respect though, I am greatly relieved that you don't know me at all.'

'That's quite all right.' Phyllis smiles. 'I fully understand. You've fallen for Lucy.'

Phyllis and Chester escort me to the threshold of the door. I say my goodbyes and when I glance back, I see Phyllis give me a wave, and Chester as ever, is loyally sitting by her side, wagging his tail.

I leave Woodchurch in high spirits but still determined to get to the bottom of this mystery, keener than ever to visit Lucy and share my findings. Surely, she will consider me now…

~Chapter 16~

November 2nd, 1945

I walk up the hill, through the tall iron gates of St Stephens Hospital and along the extended driveway.

Coming back here is strange and rather moving too, because this is where I spent months recuperating and met the lovely Nurse Brooks for the first time.

I cast my eyes up. Naturally it begins to rain, because whenever I set out on foot, it invariably rains, particularly when there is nowhere to shelter. Just my luck.

Clouds roll across the ashen sky; beads of rainwater are released and for a few moments the intensity is the type that makes rivers rise and washes debris away. Then its energy lessens but I still receive the constant heaviness of the drops.

The rain comes down sideways, full-ways and numerous other ways too, that I don't care to remember. I am soon drenched. The water drips down my neck, soaks my coat and seems to dampen my very soul.

When I enter the hospital, I take off my hat and coat, and I leave a little puddle behind me.

I walk past reception and head to Westbourne Ward.

'Mucky day,' the receptionist calls out as I pass.

On the way, I peer discreetly into an office window and see Matron sitting there. Fortunately, she doesn't see me as she is in a meeting of some kind. I inhale sharply and with head down I quicken my soggy step.

Upon seeing Nurse Grant attending to an empty bed, I stop. 'I want to talk to you about something.'

'Jack?' Nurse Grant drops a set of sheets. 'What are you doing back here?'

'I need you to explain something to me.'

Nurse Grant nervously looks up and down the ward. 'You shouldn't be in here.'

'Matron's not about,' I confirm. 'I've checked; she's in a meeting.'

'Good, she's in a sore mood today. I'm already in the soup for not changing these sheets.'

'I see.' I look at a large stack of sheets and pillow cases.

'What is it then?' she asks, setting her hands on her hips. 'And be quick!'

'It's about my haversack...'

'What about it?' Her voice tightens.

'You told me that the haversack belonged to me.'

'It does.'

'So - who does that photograph belong to, the one I found inside?'

I wait for a response. She looks to the floor and shuffles her feet.

'Well?' I ask.

She looks up and blinks, and then admits, 'It was me who slipped that picture into the bag.'

'Why?'

Nurse Grant shrugs. 'I don't know, really.'

I sigh in a pronounced way. 'Why on earth you would do that?'

'I suppose, if I'm honest, I felt a little sorry for you.'

'So, you put an anonymous picture in my belongings to, what, cheer me up?'

'How can I explain,' she says sheepishly, 'I knew that you would be excited to receive your belongings and potentially find out who you were...'

'...When I peeked inside your case, disappointingly there... there was nothing much in it at all.'

'Why did you give me something that wasn't mine?'

'It was an idea I had at the time of your dark thoughts…'

My suicidal thoughts?

'…I thought if I could give you something - or rather someone - to live for, it might help you.' She sighs. 'Matron wouldn't have exactly discouraged me.'

'Matron? What's she got to do with this?'

Nurse Grant purses her lips, glances up and down the ward and then meets my eye.

'Matron warned Lucy that she was getting too close to you. There are strict guidelines between staff and patients. In a way, I felt that I was helping both of you.'

'Did you write the message on the back of the photograph?'

Nurse Grant shrinks back into her shell. I study her well-scrubbed, shiny face and wait.

'In hindsight it seems a terrible idea,' she continues reluctantly, 'but Lucy could have been fired and you know full well we were losing you.'

'So, you think it is a good idea to switch belongings to cheer people up?'

'Just you, to cheer you up. I haven't done this before, you know.'

I turn to leave, and then turn back.

'How can you play with someone's life like that?'

'I meant no harm. Honestly.'

I kick my heels. 'I suppose you didn't,' I concede. 'You were only trying to help me. I can see that.'

'Of course I was,' she says, and appears visibly troubled. 'We thought you might even be suicidal, for bally sake.'

I shake my head back and forth and recall my former state of mind.

'I didn't want to be moved to rehabilitation. I knew that I wouldn't be able to see Lucy anymore. I was lost. I'm greatly embarrassed to say, I'd given up all hope.'

'But how did you find out that the picture was a fake?' Nurse Grant asks me.

'I've recently traced the woman in the photograph. Naturally, she's never seen me before. Lucy still thinks that this woman - Phyllis - was my girlfriend.'

'Well, I am truly sorry about that. But there's no harm done, is there? You'll soon forget about it.'

'You don't understand,' I say in an effort to explain. 'I've fallen in love with Lucy – and this woman has been the wedge in the possibility of any kind of relationship with Lucy.'

'Oh.' Nurse Grant stands motionless, unsure of what to do or say.

'I have to find her.' I vow.

'Listen,' she says after a while. 'I'll take you to her; we'll straighten this whole mess out.'

'Let's go,' I urge.

'I can't leave just yet. Meet me in an hour, when I have a break.'

'Where?'

'Norton's café; it's just across from the road from the hospital.'

'I know it.' I glance at my watch. 'See you in an hour then.'

She gives me a rushed wave and turns back to her work.

'Do you mind if I say hello to a couple of patients?' I ask before I go.

'That should be fine but...'

'I know - be quick,' I say. 'I will.'

One by one, I go over to a few patients I recognise from my stay in the ward. I make some small-talk and we have a little catch-up while Matron is gone.

I make my exit and even though I do not work at the hospital - and I have been to war - Matron still scares me a little; perish the thought if she were to catch me wandering around her wards, uninvited and dripping on her pristine floors.

~Chapter 17~

I wait, restless, in the little café where we have arranged to meet, drinking lukewarm coffee and smoking like a distressed chimney.

At the appointed time, Nurse Grant appears in the doorway and beckons to me. I stub out my latest smoke in the full ashtray on the table.

'Where are we going?' I ask.

'To my quarters,' Nurse Grant says. 'We share.'

'You and Lucy?'

She nods.

I raise an eyebrow and mutter my thanks.

'It's not far,' she says as she leads me away.

I follow Nurse Grant to a white stuccoed building: the nurses' block which is set back in the rural grounds of the hospital.

Upon entering, we walk along a badly-lit corridor, 'You shouldn't really be here,' she says. 'I'll sneak you in.'

'Lucy?' she calls out as she enters the room but there is no reply. Nurse Grant calls back to me. 'Come in, Jack.'

I raise an eyebrow at the sparse and rather cramped accommodation; it is little more than a couple of beds, an appointed kitchenette and a washbasin in another corner.

'It's a good arrangement,' she assures me, 'I work days generally and Lucy works the night shift. She'll probably be back in a moment. Do you want to wait a few minutes?'

Nurse Grant appears mindful of the passing time and of her impending return to the hospital.

'Cup of tea? She offers and glances at her watch again. 'I've got ten minutes.'

'No thanks,' I say, frustrated that Lucy isn't here.

'It's nice to see you looking better,' Nurse Grant says. 'I'm pleased.'

'How about you?' I ask. 'Are you doing all right?'

She forces a smile. 'Not too bad'

Nurse Grant sits down on the edge of the bed, takes a packet of cigarettes from her handbag and offers me one. I raise my hand.

'I'm trying to quit.'

'Oh,' she says, 'How's that going?'

'Not very well.'

She gives an empathetic smile. 'Me too.'

I then try to relax and attempt small-talk,

'Why do you do it,' I ask, 'for such little gain?'

'Nursing? I'm proud to do my bit. I'm proud of being a nurse at St Stephens. I want to help the wounded, and, like you, I'm patriotic too. So, there is plenty of gain, just by giving.'

I nod. 'Of course. I think you are all amazing. I don't know how you do it really.'

She shrugs modestly, crosses her legs and lights up. As she starts puffing on her cigarette, I keep my eyes anxiously peeled on the door.

'I'm sure she'll be back soon,' she reassures me, now puffing on the cigarette as if smoking a cigar.

She catches my eye.

'How is Harry?' she asks.

'Harry Barnes?' I ask in disbelief.

She nods. 'The one and the same.'

'He's okay, I think.' I shrug. 'Why?'

'I went on a blind date with him once.'

'Seriously?'

'Mm-hmm… Lucy arranged it.'

'Lucy did?' I wonder how that was possible. 'Lucy set you up on a date with Harry?'

'Humph.' She rolls her eyes. 'Yes, she did.'

'Well, what did you make of Harry? He is a bit shy after all,' I joke.

'He certainly wasn't shy. In fact, he was quite forward.' She laughs. 'I like him all right but I never heard from him again.'

'That sounds like Harry.' I nod in sympathy as I try to picture the two of them together.

I am still curious as to how Lucy knows Harry and the fact that she has never mentioned him. There had been a curious moment when they first met… I give up on the idea as my head begins to spin.

I indicate the wardrobes. 'So, which is Lucy's?'

She points to a particular wardrobe, which I immediately open. I return a surprised expression.

'That's funny,' she says, jumping up. 'Her clothes are all gone.'

'By the looks of things so has she,' I say, turning to the made-up bed.

'I can't believe it.'

I frown. 'Where do you think she is?'

'I've no idea. She was here, sleeping when I left for my shift at 6.00 a.m., I don't understand it.'

Nurse Grant sits back down, reflective, and stares into space. Then she turns her neck which becomes frozen and tilted at an angle. I follow her newly-concentrated eye line. Across from her, something is secreted between the mattress and the base of the bed.

'What is it?' I ask.

She balances her cigarette on the edge of the ashtray, reaches over and extracts the object from the bed. 'This may have been left for you.'

'What is it?'

'Lucy's diary,' she guesses. 'Or a journal of some sort.'

'Oh,' I stutter. 'Is there anything inside?'

Nurse Grant scans the handwritten entries in blue ink and answers in the affirmative.

I rub my chin and, starting to feel intrusive, I decide to leave.

'Are you going to give up?' Nurse Grant asks in surprise. 'Just like that?'

I turn back and half-croak. 'What can I do?'

'You love her, don't you?'

'I do.'

'You know Lucy likes you.'

'I once thought she did,' I admit, 'but now I'm not so sure.'

Nurse Grant pitches the journal to me. 'Here - you'd better read this if you want to find her.'

'Why? Have you read it?'

She shakes her head. 'I don't need to; I can guess what's in there. You see, we had a bit of a falling out.'

'Did you?' I ask in surprise.

'Inconsequential stuff, that's all. I think it was about using the last bar of soap, or something daft like that. There's a lot of pressure and we're all tired. Lucy is lovely, actually.'

I smile in agreement. 'I know she is.'

I hesitantly take the journal and then sigh. 'I can't read this - it wouldn't be right.'

'She probably left it here for you.'

'Why would she do that?'

Nurse Grant taps her foot impatiently. 'To help you find her.'

'But she'd never forgive me for reading it.'

'She'd never forgive herself if you didn't read it.'

I have no clue what Nurse Grant is talking about.

'I have to get back to work,' she says, 'otherwise Matron will be after me.'

I grimace. 'Ah, Matron - did she get out of bed on the wrong side again?'

'Matron's all right really. She's just doing her job.'

'She always seemed to have it in for me.'

'She's tough but fair. Everyone will tell you that.'

'Sorry. I didn't mean to sound harsh.'

'And I'm sorry too,' Nurse Grant says. 'I hope I haven't messed things up for you two. I meant well, really, I did. I hope you can find her.'

I bat away her apology. 'You meant well, I'm sure.'

Nurse Grant finishes up her cigarette and fiercely stubs it out in the ashtray. 'Read it,' she orders, indicating the journal.

I examine the leather cover and tilt my head, half in despair and half in impending guilt.

'Turn the light off and shut the door when you leave,' she instructs, glancing at her watch.

I sit down on the bed for a moment. My head is aching and I'm in need of some fresh air.

Leaving with the journal still in my hand, I chance upon the Smith's Arms off the high street.

After I order a pint of beer, I drop a shilling on the bar, push Lucy's journal under my armpit and carry the glass to a dingy corner of the lounge. Finding a small table, I sit down.

Then I lightly run my finger along the spine and imagine all of the times Lucy has held it.

I turn the journal over and study the gold clasp that I am contemplating opening. I have taken Nurse Grant's advice to read it.

I mutter 'Please forgive me for what I am about to do, but this might be the only way I can find you, Lucy.'

Nervously, I unclench my hand and open the fastening.

~*Part 3*~

~Chapter 18~

Once I open Lucy's journal, it is obvious that it is, indeed, a diary, with pages set out for daily entries.

I notice it is blank from January right the way through to May. Slightly apprehensive, I take my glasses from a case and stop at the first entry in June. The writing is ragged and inconsistent, neat lines of writing often deteriorating into a scrawl. I start reading the first entry.

Diary Entry: 10th June, 1944

I have searched everywhere for Jack. I have searched in hospitals, hostels, homes and even a graveyard.
Since the telegram listed Jack as 'missing in action', I have been in utter turmoil and have told my family and friends that I will not

give up until I find Jack, whether I find him dead or somehow wonderfully and miraculously alive; I will not leave any stone unturned. I will contact the 1st Dorsets Regiment and talk to returning soldiers if I can.

I believe Jack is still alive... I don't know why, but I sense he came back from France and somewhere he needs me and is waiting for me. Probably, all families might say that about their lost ones, but I can only go on my intuition. Possibly, it is a fond hope but I do have hope at least.

I pause, sit back and take a deep breath.

It doesn't make sense...

I re-read the passage and mumble to myself: 'Lucy was searching for me?'

I sit there in a daze for a moment, back-tracking every memory and every encounter I've had with Lucy; I am still incredulous to learn that she might have known me all along.

I recall our long chats in the ward at night, when she would discreetly pull up a chair and talk with me.

I remember that she was the first person I saw when I awoke from my coma and that she told me my name was Jack. She was the only person who must have known.

I can picture her winking and smiling to me from across the ward, and remember countless endearing interactions with her, and the many kindnesses she has shown towards me. She has found me and was helping me all of this time.

It does make sense...

~Chapter 19~

Diary Entry: 28th June, 1944

I turn the pages and run my eye down various lists - all set out like shopping lists - but they are full of hospitals and various rehabilitation and military care establishments.

By each name there is either a comment i.e. 'no luck', 'no', or mostly the name is simply crossed out.

Numerous pages later, I stop on an entry for 28th June where there is a more detailed account.

Having visited countless hospitals, I had some hope today.
I was told at the reception desk of St Stephen's Hospital in Bournemouth, that there is a serviceman who was rescued from the Normandy beaches and he is presently in a coma. He has no

identification whatsoever. He has been badly wounded and they say he has a long recovery ahead of him.

I begged to be taken to the ward to see if it might be Jack. Nervously, I walked the final few steps to the bed because I had done this countless times before and been disappointed.

I peered at a pale and thin face, half-submerged in the pillow, his eyes were firmly closed. My very first glance revealed I had found my Jack!

I glanced back at the clerk because I wanted to shriek with joy but instead, I started crying quietly. She left me alone and I sat down beside him. I talked to Jack for a while but of course he could not respond. However, I prayed that he might have been able to hear my joy, my relief and my voice. I tried to give him some reassuring words.

I studied Jack's ghostly appearance, his face was so white and although he was lifeless, he was alive… I wiped my fiancée's brow, touched his cheek and kissed his forehead before I left for the night.

I am overjoyed that I can be there for him. (Jack does not have any immediate family. Both of his parents have passed away and he has no siblings).

Still giddy with excitement, I had a little money to book into a bed & breakfast in a cheaper district.

At first, I was unsure of how I could help Jack and afford to stay in close proximity, but I have had an idea that might just work. It's worth a try at least…

~Chapter 20~

29th June

Dr Berger, a Belgian national, is one of the medical specialists, and of high ranking at the hospital; this is when I had my first bit of luck. Dr Berger gave me five minutes of his time. He is slightly eccentric, not officious at all, and open to suggestions, even from a flighty young woman!

I asked Doctor Berger for a favour. I told him that I had worked as a volunteer for the Red Cross (which is perfectly true, and of course every hospital is in dire need of nurses), and that I was also the fiancée of his patient: Jack Edwards. He considered this for less than a second and then clicked his fingers as if he had thought up the whole idea!

He said he would arrange for me to attend a 12-week training course, during which I would be a probationer and work some practical time in the wards as an assistant.

He told me that Jack had amnesia: a memory disorder, and that he was conscious at one point but did not recall anything, not even his own name and that after his operation, he fell into a coma.

There is one caveat: If Jack has temporary memory loss - which can happen in shell-shock cases - he said I must not reveal to Jack who I am, not yet at least. He said that Jack must remember by himself, and he undoubtedly will, he assured me.

Also, working in the same ward as a loved-one is not standard practice and revealing my relationship would curtail my opportunity to help and be near to Jack.

I must promise to be discreet because no one must know of our connection. Dr Berger said, 'How does that saying go? Keep it under your hat? Then you must do that.'

I replied that I would keep it between 'you, me and the gate-post' - and he said, 'I'd prefer it if the gate-post didn't know.'

He was so helpful and funny.

I also promised to help and care for all of my future patients. Of course, I will! I literally raised my shaking hand and made a vow.

'Best of luck to your Jack,' he said, 'I will do what I can to help him.'

He asked my name and he smiled, 'Welcome to St Stephens, Nurse Brooks.'

I sit back again bewildered and bemused: *my fiancée?* I briefly look up and across to the other patrons. With my beer still untouched, I read on.

***

Diary Entry: July 25th, 1944

Wonderful news!

From across the ward, I caught sight of Jack's head move back and forth, so, full of hope, I went and sat at his bedside and held his hand. After a while I noticed his eyelids flicker.

Jack responded and just like that, he opened his eyes. He said nothing and sadly, there seemed to be no recognition on his part; he just peered helplessly into my eyes. Poor thing.

He tried to say something but no words would come. I simply told him he was in hospital, had been in a coma and that I would take care of him. I informed him of his true name: Jack. Shortly after that, he closed his eyes.

~Chapter 21~

Diary Entry: 6th August, 1944

I am now working in Westbourne Ward or more importantly - Jack's ward. This wing of the hospital is for convalescing patients. When they are strong enough and they have been through some rehabilitation, they will move on.

It is wonderful to be so close to him.

I took a great risk today and propped my head next to his, as he was sleeping. I couldn't resist because I just had to be near to him. After a few minutes he seemed to be waking so I returned to the office. Right now, however, Jack is the least of my worries.

I am immersed with my training and extra studies and, due to lack of sleep, I am always tired. Nursing is demanding and it is a whole new world to me. It's certainly not for the faint of heart either, as some of the injuries I have already seen are quite severe.

My colleagues are all so dedicated and Matron suffers fools badly. I cannot afford any slip-ups. I do feel useful however, and I am proud to be making a contribution to the war effort.

There are so many rules to follow, so much to learn and I quickly realise everything is based on seniority.

Matron is very strict and casts her sharp eye about in expectations of highly-polished clean wards, beds made-up with crisp, crease-free sheets and everything scrubbed within an inch of its life.

She issues a list of personal rules we must follow religiously.

We must wear low-heel shoes, no make-up, have short nails, hair must not reach the collar, and when on duty we must wear black stockings with no ladders in them. We also must open doors for doctors, stand when a senior member of staff enters the room, and never run, except in the case of fire.

At the end of my shift, I often unwind in the nurses' lounge and join my colleagues who might be listening to the news on the radio, playing cards or just chatting.

When on day shift, nurses must be in bed by 10.00 p.m. The night sister comes around to check the bedrooms and then locks the front door! (There is a fire escape for those who dare use it although I have no reason to!).

I am told that I get one half day off a week and one full day off a month!

~Chapter 22~

I am ecstatic that Jack has woken up, but I did not share my emotions with Nurse Grant, or with Matron. Of course, I informed them of the fact and kept my emotions on an even keel. Just.

I am moving along with my training and now working the night shift so that I am able to spend more time with my Jack.

One evening when he seemed low in spirits, I opened the office door, so that he could hear the radio. I know he used to love listening to music, sometimes jazz, but particularly classical, so I found a station and turned the volume up. I know he enjoyed it because I caught a glimmer of pleasure on his face!

Jack appears lost at times and when his eyes are not following me, he's staring out of the window. Sometimes those eyes seem haunted and I'm still not sure if it is a result of his war experience, or if he is trying to recall his past.

Just as the doctor had feared, Jack has lost his memory. He has, however, shared a small flashback memory - or flashbulb memory, I think Dr Bergen calls it - of meeting me at the Station Café before he was dispatched to France. Though he cannot see my face in the memory.

I will try to coax him along slowly and prompt him with his recollections. He has flirted non-stop today and has already asked me out, which on one hand is flattering but in a strange way it seems disloyal to his 'old' girlfriend - me! I do forgive him though.

~Chapter 23~

Diary Entry: 5th September, 1944

Today Jack gave me a flower that he picked from the hospital's courtyard. I know the lengths he went to, to find it, flinging himself from his wheelchair and literally crawling to the flowerbed.

I watched the incredible scene play out from a stairwell window. Fortunately, an orderly was passing and came to his rescue. I pretended not to have seen him, to spare his dignity. I wasn't fully sure what he was doing until much later.

When Jack gave the flower to me, the gesture overwhelmed me and I started to cry.

To tell the truth, I'm not even sure why I became so emotional. I made an excuse about the war getting to me although he was still perplexed. The secrecy is killing me inside and I want to talk to Jack so badly; hugging him helped, but today was one of my toughest days at St Stephens.

I think I might have been too hard on Jack. I have almost bullied him into remembering me. If he falls for me - and I think he is doing so all over again - he will surely never remember.

He has had a few more flashbacks but nothing very helpful. Depression has set in, and there have been signs that he has contemplated taking his own life; not a serious attempt as yet, but the ward nurses are worried about him too. He is on the 'watch list' as we call it.

~Chapter 24~

Diary Entry: 12th September, 1944

Jack has been placed temporarily in a private room. He has been depressed; we are worried about his well-being. Oh Jack... I thought you were improving and ready to move on.

Nurse Grant gave me Jack's haversack today. I recognized almost everything inside, and I knew it was his, so, excitedly, I went to him with it.

For some reason the clasp was jammed and when he went to open it, Jack was reminded of his missing arm. I tried not to show any emotion, I am trying to be strong for him, but I started welling up and nearly cried, not out of pity, but because of his disappointment at not being able to carry out a simple task. In front of me, he seemed to think he was less of a man.

As we pulled out the items one by one, I desperately tried to jog his memory, because there was the theatre ticket for Gracie Fields (which he couldn't remember our going to) and there was the little book I had given him... I cajoled and prompted him, but to no avail.

Then something shocking occurred: inside the bag was a photograph. It was of a beautiful woman and, to cap it all, had a message for Jack on the back. How does that old saying go? 'Sticks and stones can break your bones but words can never harm you.' Well, I would take the sticks and stones because the words were like daggers to my heart, words that I can never forget:

"To Jack, my sweetheart: You are my love, my life for always. I love you." Followed by three kisses.

My stomach tightened, my heart did somersaults and my head became dizzy. It hadn't occurred to me that Jack might have had a girlfriend; somebody else aside from me. Why would it? We were, and still are, technically, engaged - for God's sake! How long could it have been going on?

Naturally, I am jealous and upset all at the same time - cheating is cheating - but I had to make light of it, even imitating the three kisses, but it stuck in my throat. I had even worn his favourite perfume (Matron scolded me and instructed me never to wear perfume while on duty); anyway, Jack failed to remember that too - although he said he liked it.

All I could do was pack the bag away and leave as fast as I could. I went straight to the toilet and cried and cried. After a while, Matron knocked on the door. I told her I felt sick with a 'stomach bug' and she sent me home with a firm, 'Be sure to be here at 6.00 a.m. tomorrow!'

~Chapter 25~

Diary Entry for: 22nd October, 1944

Jack leaves in a week. I still love him but it appears that he might have cheated on me.

I am in shock and flit between fighting for him one minute and letting him go the next. I notice that Nurse Grant has put 'that' picture in a frame and has set it on Jack's bedside table. As I really was sick and nauseous, I volunteered my services in another ward where they were short-staffed. When I returned, I noticed that Jack, bless him, had taken down the picture of the attractive woman, his girlfriend. I am so confused!

Do I still want Jack to remember his past and subsequently remember this other woman? What if he doesn't remember at all? Isn't what Jack and I have - in the present - good enough?

He seems to have no recollection of 'that' woman but he can't remember me either. I am in a love triangle and I might be the only one who knows about it!

What do I do? I could tell Jack but I have made a promise to Dr Berger, and if Matron learns of my secret, I will be cast aside forever.

~Chapter 26~

28th September, 1944

R.I.P. Nurse Ruth Gibbs. 1916-1944

This was the saddest and my most desperate day at St Stephens. Last night, Nurse Gibbs was murdered; she lost her life for being in the wrong place at the wrong time. It could have been any of us working the shift in Westbourne Ward. It just happened to be her, but how brave she was to have resisted the intruder.

We held a minute's silence for her at 12.00 noon today. The nurses, usually so stoic, were in tears in the nurses' lounge. Even Matron was teary-eyed for a while before rallying.

We have become like family and to lose one of our own is hard to bear. It is so senseless.

We await details of her funeral when we will try to provide comfort and support for her family.

Today, tearfully, I dedicated my nursing efforts to her memory.

~Chapter 27~

4th May, 1944

The end of the war is just days away - or so they say on the radio and it's all over the newspapers.
I have written a note to Jack encouraging him to celebrate and enjoy himself. If anyone needs to, he does.

8th May, 1945

Day Shift.

Today, we were allowed to set up a radio for patients and staff in the ward to hear the Prime Minister, Winston Churchill address the nation. He declared that Germany had surrendered. The war in Europe really is over!

The BBC reported that The Prime Minister was mobbed by excited crowds as he made his way from Downing Street to the House of Commons.

After his speech, loud cheering could be heard throughout the hospital. Matron turned a blind eye to a few celebratory drinks with patients and staff and, once the party atmosphere faded, we carried on with our work. I think I had an extra bounce in my step during my shift. I think we all did, and even the patients were greatly cheered.

It isn't until now, sitting here, that I can reflect upon the meaning of the news and think about the sacrifices made.

Strangely, I am walking out of a six-year fog and I now must rebuild my life. Nothing will be the same for any of us.

We have all lost loved ones; we have all made sacrifices and we have all shed tears.

Later…

The nurses had a little get-together and a celebratory drink in the lounge this evening. Afterwards, on a whim, and being so lonely, I decided I wanted to be with Jack.

I visited some of the public houses of Bournemouth in hopes of finding him. Fortunately, there weren't too many, but they were all very lively, and the celebrations were already in full swing. Each public house was packed to the rafters.

When I entered the Kings Head, I could see Jack propped up by the bar. He was the worse for wear and had taken my advice to the letter to enjoy himself. He didn't see me, so I stood around like his unseen angel (or his guardian angel as it turned out on this occasion).

A little while later he slumped to the floor. Panicked, I made my way over to him, but he was out cold. With the help of his buddies, we bundled him out of the pub and into a taxi. Getting in, I asked the driver to take him to the shelter, Bear Cross House on Carlton Avenue.

I called back from the taxi window and encouraged his friends to carry on with their revelries, assuring them that I would take care of him. In reality, I couldn't and the taxi driver had to help pick him up. Between us, we somehow carried him indoors. (Luckily Jack hadn't lost his key, so I was able to access his room).

In the hallway, a resident stopped by Jack's still-open doorway. The man had a line of bunting wrapped around his waist, a little cocktail umbrella behind one ear and streamers around his neck. When he came in, he blew on the party horn still in his mouth, which squeaked and unrolled towards me.

I smiled and introduced myself, informing him that I was Jack's friend.

He took the horn from his mouth, theatrically removed his beret, tucking it under his armpit, and then bowed - as if meeting Royalty. He then took my right hand and kissed the back of it. 'It's a great pleasure to meet you.'

I learnt that he was called Harry, Jack's neighbour.

Harry scrutinized his unconscious friend.

'Is he all right?' he asked.

'Yes, he's just resting.'

'Do you like Jack?' I asked.

'Of course, he's a good egg.'

'He needs a good friend…'

'I'm his best friend,' he said, 'although, he may not know it yet.' He then cocked his head to one side. 'You're the nurse, aren't you?'

'Yes.' I nodded. 'Has Jack ever told you anything about me?' I asked him.

He grinned back and said, 'Everything', adding, 'You're the complicated one.'

'He said that?'

Harry gave me a huge smile. 'He did.'

'You must promise not to tell him you've seen me, complicated or not.'

He scratched the side of his head and turned back to Jack. 'Now look here, that's a bit of a tall order. Jack is a pal of mine.'

'I know, your best friend,' I reminded him. *'I'm glad of that, truly I am. But is there anything I can do for you in return?'* I asked. *(Ironically, I'm the one suggesting he should blackmail me - ha!).*

Harry swung around.

'Well, it seems an innocent request, well, let me think... Jack did say you might line me up with a date with one of your nurse friends.'

'Did he?'

We both watched over Jack for a moment as he slept.

Harry shifted his feet. He didn't look me in the eye, I noticed.

'Okay, I think I could arrange that.'

'Do you have someone in mind?'

'I think I do.'

(Truth was I didn't have anyone in mind!).

'Is she nice?'

'Very.'

'Pretty?'

'Of course.'

Harry beamed. He made a motion of zipping up his lips and turned on his heel to leave.

I stepped into the hallway to watch Harry perform a funny little hop and skip as he went along.

What with the lateness of the hour I presumed Harry would be off to bed after that, but surprisingly he left again by the front door.

What a funny fellow he was…

Periodically through-out the night I checked on Jack and made sure he was okay. In the end, I fell asleep on his settee and when early morning came, I quietly let myself out, with Jack being none the wiser.

***

12th May, 1945

Jack has called three times and written two notes to me in the last two weeks. Each time he has invited me to either tea, coffee, the pictures or dinner. I suppose a promise is a promise. I am torn about our situation but I accepted his invitation, played safe and chose to have tea with him.

~Chapter 28~

Diary Entry: 20th May, 1945

I met Jack today. He was fetching in his suit and tie, and of course he was as polite and charming as ever. On the other hand, I was as late as ever. Oh dear!

He gave me a single rose - he is still a hopeless romantic (just like me, of course).

We had a pleasant tea together and I could tell he was nervous, wanting to make a good impression with me. In truth he probably wasn't as nervous as I was; my heart was thumping away.

Funny though, whenever we meet and talk, we soon laugh together and all our nervousness quickly disappears.

He seemed particularly enamoured of me. His eyes were firmly fixed on me and he rarely even blinked! Bless him.

It's true, I had made a great effort as it was his first time (that he can remember...) seeing me in civvies and not in uniform. Besides, make-up is becoming more accessible again. So, I have a good excuse.

I asked him about his memory but he said he hadn't recalled anything (except for an angel called Nurse Brooks - which was sweet). We walked along the pier and we kissed. I felt confused and wasn't sure what to do after that: should I take the plunge or hold back? I decided the latter.

I still want Jack to remember his past and, when he does, at least he will be able to choose whom he wants to be with. I suppose I am as confused as he is, but our day together was wonderful: walking arm in arm, it felt like the old days again, when we really were a couple.

When I asked Jack about his hopes and wishes, he declared 'To have someone to love, to care for, and to grow old with.' My sentiments and wishes exactly.

I had my bit of fun asking Jack about VE Day; he sensed I knew something but wasn't telling. I was able to deflect his interest and playfully resisted his probing.

Which reminded me; I had a promise to keep: a date for Harry? I glanced about the nurse's sitting room and all of them either had boyfriends or were engaged to be married. As if right under my nose, my roommate appeared: Nurse Grant. She is single and was suitably enthusiastic to go on a (blind) date. I spread it on a bit thick, if not exactly gilding the lily, regarding Harry. I hope she will still speak to me after meeting him! He will no doubt, make an impression on her, if nothing else!

I will set up the date for next week. He has given me his phone number, so I can call him with the exciting news.

Jack is different in some ways. He has become more independent; he is overcoming his disability and doesn't appear to feel sorry for himself at all. I would say the shelter has been good for him. Jack still has his sense of humour and his kind and considerate ways are to the fore: little things like pulling out my chair for me when I sit down, giving me his jacket when I am cold and complimenting my perfume and clothes. He is very charming.

I sat on the train afterwards - with his silver florin in my hand - and relived the day with Jack over and over again in my mind. It had been in some ways a perfect day.

Part of me wished I had chosen all four invitations, including the dinner invitation and going to the pictures. I am so stupid at times! I must work on being more spontaneous.

~Chapter 29~

I skip through a number of sporadic entries over the next few months, until I see a date that is significant: the last time I saw Lucy...

Diary Entry: October 25th, 1945

I have been thinking constantly about Jack and I have found myself unconsciously rolling that florin around in my hand. I initially wanted to give him some space to find himself - and I have been so busy at the hospital - but I couldn't bear to be apart from him anymore, and I finally succumbed.

I wondered if his memory had returned in the interim. Supposing I showed up and his W.A.A.F. girlfriend was there? I couldn't compete with her, besides it would have been downright awkward.

I invented a few scenarios in my head, a series of excuses if she happened to be there when I rang his doorbell, just in case...

I could be his long-lost cousin, alternatively, I could be answering an advert he had placed for a domestic helper or something, or maybe I could be following-up on his progress on behalf of St Stephens. Perhaps all ludicrous ideas and worries...

The reality was that I saw him sitting idly and out-of-sorts in the bay of the window with the usual cigarette in his mouth. He was on his own and, I confess, I had have never felt so relieved - and happy she wasn't there.

When he saw me I noticed his eyes light up, and he was suddenly full of cheer and optimism. Perhaps we really are meant to be together because I felt exactly the same way too.

I planned on telling him about us, about everything, but when the time came, I was too nervous, had second thoughts about it all and couldn't do it. Don't ask me why. Perhaps the longer you leave telling the truth the harder it becomes. I think there is something of that in my predicament - that, and the other woman from his past.

I tried to get some answers from him but he still could not remember his past and is convinced he never will.

There was one slightly awkward moment during my visit: Harry came round. We pretended not to have met before, although Harry said something daft. What was it? Oh yes, when introduced he said, 'You're quite a beauty in the daylight.' Silly, great fool that he is!

We muddled through it and I don't think Jack was any the wiser.

I mentioned Nurse Grant's name - I had set him up on a date with her - and he shifted uneasily because the cad hadn't bothered to call her back. Oh Harry, you are a disappointment!

Anyway, I was exhausted from my night shift and almost immediately I fell asleep on Jack's settee (again). What must he have thought? When I awoke, he was sipping a beer and watching over me. He said he had still enjoyed my company. He can be so sweet sometimes. I hope I didn't talk in my sleep!

I think Jack is in love with me but my affection for him is more complicated. I left no clearer about things than when I arrived.

~Chapter 30~

November 1st, 1945

After much deliberation, I have decided to return home. I have been back and forth over my situation. My goal was to find Jack and I have achieved that, I have helped nurse him back to health and he is now back on his own two feet.

I went to see Dr Berger today to thank him for allowing me to work at St Stephens Hospital, and for giving me the opportunity to become a nurse.

Dr Berger was in the midst of packing his office up. He told me he was flying back to Belgium tomorrow to return home.

I told him that I am going to transfer to my hometown, ideally work in the local hospital where I can be nearer to my family. I have started a career that I love and wish to pursue. He asked about Jack, and I told him that I hoped he would join me one day.

He wished me luck and said, 'It's a new chapter for both of us!'

I spoke to Matron who said she was sorry to see me go. I told her that I hoped to continue nursing.

In true form, she listed the things I should remember not to do - which included not to' wear perfume, make-up or get too close to your patients.' She sent me away with a ringing endorsement, 'You're a good nurse and a good girl, Nurse Brooks. Good luck!'

This, coming from her, made me feel ten foot tall! I walked out of the hospital after my last shift with a glow of pride and a modest amount of satisfaction: I did it!

I am leaving us - Jack and me - in 'the lap of the gods' or rather to fate and, most importantly, to Jack. One day, I know that he will remember and he must decide with whom he wants to make a life, I have done all that I can.

***

I turn the page and realise it is the last entry. I check the date; the entry was written yesterday!

Flattened between the next two pages is the forget-me-not, the flower from the courtyard that I gave Lucy all that time ago.

When I inspect the page more closely, I can see that it is all spoilt from water - or more likely, I wonder, from tear-stains.

I find a photograph of me tucked inside the very next page. I am pictured leaning against an old Triumph motorcycle wearing a tweed cap, a cream V-neck sweater under leather jacket and wide trousers with brown lace-up boots.

I view the face, it is undeniably me, but I seem to be a different person, someone without a care in the world. I stare at the image in a mixture of surprise and lament.

How I wish I could be transported back in time to that innocent moment and, most importantly, be there with Lucy by my side.

I snap the diary shut.

~Part 4~

~Chapter 31~

The past has been haunting me but now it invigorates me. The trouble is, I still don't know where to start, and I am scratching my head slightly over it all.

Distracted, I raise my head to see a few working men, I'm guessing machine operators or mechanics, in overalls, talking and drinking animatedly, all in good humour. One of them has noticed my reddened, slapped face of an expression.

'Cheer up mate, it may never happen.'

I smile back glumly. 'It already has.'

How anyone can rejoice or laugh at a time like this seems impossible, but of course they aren't in my predicament, and I am unable to raise a smile.

I close up the diary, place it down on the table and when I look up again the barman gives me a wave.

I go over. 'What is it?' I ask full of curiosity.

'For you,' he says, pushing a brandy towards me. 'That fella' over there bought it for you.'

I see the man, the one who shared a few words with me, moments earlier. I pick the drink up, hold it high and - making sure he can see my gratitude - I toast his good health.

The man gives me a good-natured thumbs up. I immediately sink the brandy and reflect upon his kindness; it seems to me that there is still plenty of it about, despite the hardships and austerity that still exist. I make a vow to pass on his goodwill.

My thoughts return to Lucy and the revelations in her diary. I have always sensed there was a connection between us, but I hadn't realized that our connection went back to before my time in hospital. To be honest, I am still astounded by the revelations.

As I sit and drink I try to let it all sink in…

~Chapter 32~

I return to Bear Cross House, take off my jacket and pour myself a drink. After a few sips, I walk the length of my sitting room, up and down, up and down I pace. I then knock loudly once on the adjoining wall.

'What is it this time?' Harry gasps a few seconds later as he rushes in my front door. 'A relapse?'

'No, I need to find a girl.'

Harry slumps down in a chair and with tired eyes glances over to the wall. 'We're not really following the code anymore, are we?'

'This is an emergency too,' I assure him.

'Ah!' he exclaims, 'don't tell me: the complicated one.'

'How did you know?'

'I told you already; I'm au fait with these sorts of things. Is it the nurse?'

'Of course, Lucy. I could do with your help.'

'Help with a girl? Let me see...' He sits up and takes this as an invitation to share his thoughts on the fairer sex. He begins to wax lyrical about love, albeit if Valentino were an Englishman.

Then he says, 'Well, I'm your man of course. What do you need: A love poem written by yours truly? Some flowers? A good bottle of plonk?'

'It's going to take a lot more than that.'

'Yeah.' Harry sits back again. 'I was afraid of that.'

'Are you in?'

'In for a penny...' he says, and looks at me cautiously.

'Don't worry; it's not going to cost you any money, just time.'

'Good - you'd be welcome to every last penny; it's just that I don't have very much. So, what do you need me to do?'

I massage my temples and brush the hair back across my scalp.

'You see, Lucy has left, vanished, gone; I don't know where she is...' I pause. 'I have to find my past, every single detail. I have to find out who I am, my full name, which regiment I belonged to, and where I used to live.'

Harry raises an eyebrow. 'Anything else?'

'No, but if I can achieve that I will be able to return home and I am sure I will find Lucy. I know it.'

'I don't wish to pour cold water on your romantic escapades, old man, but what if she went away for a good reason?'

'You mean she may have gone in order to leave me?'

'I didn't say it.'

'I know she still has feelings for me.'

Harry scratches his chin self-consciously. 'How can you be so sure?'

'I read her diary.'

Harry starts back in his chair. 'Crikey - you've a nerve! You do know that a woman's diary is considered to be quite private, old man?'

'If it helps me to find Lucy, I don't care. Besides, I've learnt that Lucy knew me before I ended up in hospital. I've found out that she's actually my fiancée.'

Harry seems cross-eyed for a moment and then taps his own head (in a not-so-subtle reference to mine). 'And I suppose this is all news to you!'

'Yes.'

He gives an exaggerated shake of the shoulders as if catching a chill. 'I'd certainly like to know if I was engaged to someone. You're right; it *is* complicated.'

'So, you can see...'

'I can see all right,' Harry interrupts and smiles. 'And you'll be surprised to hear that I'm not wholly unromantic. In fact, I'd be chuffed to see you two officially reunited.'

'Thank you.'

'Don't thank me, it's just so I can get some peace from your love-sick affliction and your constant knocking on my wall.'

'So, you will help?'

'Oh, I'm just having a bit of fun - of course I will.' He comes over and gives me a great big slap on the back. 'I can recognise true love when I see it!'

'It's a weight off my mind, knowing I have your help and support.'

'Think nothing of it.'

'Thank you.'

'Say,' he says with great curiosity, 'did you ever talk to that lovely, young thing in the photograph?'

'Phyllis?'

'She's called Phyllis, is she?' He whistled softly to the ceiling.

'Yes, she is.'

'And?'

'Her picture was put in my bag in error.'

'So, she didn't know you at all?'

'No.'

'So, she isn't part of your research now?'

'No.'

'But for my research... what do you know about her?'

I smile. 'She's not married or engaged - but she is respectable!'

'What are you saying - that I'm not?'

My thoughts betray me as I stifle a smile. 'I'm just saying she's not that kind of girl.'

Harry's face is a picture of indignation. I enjoy the next moment greatly when I take out her photo and dangle it in front of his eyes.

'There you go.'

'Phyllis is for me?' he says, his eyes practically the size of tea saucers.

'Well, the photograph is for you, at least.'

'Thanks,' he beams. 'You're first rate, you are.'

'Not at all.'

Harry closely stares at the image. 'Say, is she as good as this in real life?'

'Better!' I tease.

'You have to introduce me.'

'Well, Phyllis did offer that if I ever found Lucy, she would love to meet her one day - so, I'm sure we could take an extra guest along,' I say. 'There is one other thing.'

'What's that?'

'She lost her fiancée in the war.'

'Oh. The poor, sweet thing...'

'I just thought I'd better tell you.'

'Come on!' Harry exclaims. 'We've no time to lose!'

'Where do we start?' I ask hesitantly.

'Leave that to me,' says Harry. 'I'm not just a pretty face - I'm quite resourceful.' He taps the side of his nose. 'I was in the Royal Signal Corps, you know.'

~Chapter 33~

I make enquiries at St Stephen's Hospital. Apparently, Dr Berger has just left for Belgium, and I learn that there is no forwarding address given for Nurse Brooks either.

Bitterly disappointed, I have returned home.

Later, Harry sits in my room, poised, holding a pen and paper while I recall my memories, trivial and otherwise. We have been going through various recollections like two amateur detectives working on a long-forgotten case.

'What did that railway station of yours look like?' he asks.

'This is useless,' I say. 'I've been through it in my own head a thousand times.'

The truth is, every night and every morning those memories rattle around my empty head. That is all I have.

Harry stares at me critically.

'Come on,' he urges, 'try to repeat it one more time for me, and if not for me, for Lucy.'

'And if not for Lucy, for Phyllis?' I laugh.

'A bit below the belt, old man. I'm doing this for you.'

'Sorry. I didn't mean anything by it.'

'I know,' he says. 'Look, sit back, close your eyes and try and recall those flash-backs you've had.'

'The doctor calls them flashbulb memories,' I inform him. 'I was told that the memories are seared into my brain and they are the consequence of emotionally arousing circumstances.'

'Well, we just have to unlock them for you. They're in there, once you push through that mental block,' he urges.

'You'll see. Now close your eyes and try to think of that railway station, first off.'

I do as Harry instructs and try to recall. After a few moments, I visualize the location in my mind:

I am walking towards a railway station, such a picturesque setting with the cherry blossom in full flower and hue. A low white trellis fence runs along the outside of the building where the honeysuckle grows.

The grass is manicured near the entrance and there is a small border garden with a little ornate railing enclosing a First World War memorial in the shape of a cross.

I can see a quaint booking kiosk just inside the door leading to the platforms beyond, and I can see the war campaign posters on the wall. I can even read them: 'Lend a hand on the land,' and 'Put that light out!' I stop at the entrance to the station.

I light a cigarette, glance at my watch and wait for someone.

I re-open my eyes because the memory has ended. 'I had a little success.'

'Well done.'

'Okay.'

'You said that you saw German bombers fly overhead from your train.'

'Yes, they headed for the village on a bombing raid.'

'What happened?'

'We fired at them from the train when they passed back over us.'

'Maybe we can search some records of that happening,' he suggests.

'It's certainly worth a shot.'

'Let's take a gander at that bag of yours next,' he suggests. 'May I?' Harry asks, indicating that he wants to remove everything.

'Please do.'

Harry empties the contents onto the bed.

'You won't find anything particularly interesting in there.'

'The watch?'

I shake my head.

'How about this ticket for a Gracie Fields show?'

I take the ticket and hold it between my fingers.

'Try closing your eyes again,' Harry suggests. 'Try to remember, hopefully another flashbulb memory will return.'

I follow his advice and close my eyes.

I vividly recall being in a Victorian theatre in the West End of London. The buzz of expectancy is tangible as theatre-goers, some in their evening dress, and some in uniform, sip on their cocktails and drink their beers before the show. The bell for last orders sounds.

I walk up a sweeping staircase; above me are grand chandeliers and I lightly run my hand along the wooden banister as I go.

A moment later, the reception lights flicker, signalling the imminent start of the performance. Voices hush as patrons make for their seats.

A woman in front grabs my hand tightly. She giggles as we rush up the lush carpet to our seats in giddy excitement and anticipation.

Just as we go on through the curtain, in the darkness, she turns back and kisses me.

I open my eyes because it is as if a film I was watching has come to an end. I share my experience with Harry.

'I sense that my flashbulb memories really are starting to return.'

'I don't think those are flashbulb memories,' Harry says. 'I would guess that they're just regular, everyday memories.'

'I do believe my memory is starting to return then.'

'You're making good progress. Let's keep at it.'

It is stop-start after that. Harry does have one more suggestion, the one we eventually act upon.

He pours me a glass of beer. 'I have a thought.'

'What is it?' I ask swiftly, eager to know.

'We might be able to take you back in time, or at least to the place where you were most likely stationed.'

'What are you talking about?'

'Before you were shipped to Normandy. There are a few places your unit would most likely have left from, somewhere along the south coast.'

A light went on in my head. 'I see where you're going.'

'We need to pick out one or two and visit them,' he says. 'Then we'll be in business.'

~Chapter 34~

We arrive in Portsmouth and check in to the Beachcomber Hotel. When we meet up again, Harry joins me on the terrace by a set of French doors. I light up a cigarette and regard the deepening sunset.

In the stiff air, my senses are immediately heightened; the wind carries the smell of the sea and I turn my head to the seagulls crying way above me. Although getting late, the light has not quite diminished, and the skyline is full of colours one might see in the dying embers of a fire.

As I gaze out, Harry gazes back at me in awe, studying my expression.

'You remember it, don't you?' he says.
I nod. 'I do.'
'Tell me about it.'

I sit down on a low retaining wall. Harry joins me. I take a moment to get my bearings; my recollections have slowly come into sharpness like the focussing screen of a camera.

Harry sits waiting expectantly.

'Before D-Day...' I start, 'I can remember my camp being in Southsea and training there for many weeks.' I point out the location.

'I suppose the planning had been going on for some months before even we arrive. The camp was set behind barbed wire and armed guards patrolled the camps day and night. At first, we were free to come and go - in the evenings at least - and there were thousands of soldiers everywhere in the town...

...Then suddenly the camps were sealed and no-one could enter or leave because we were about to receive our instructions. We already knew that it was an enormous military operation, the biggest ever to leave from these shores, so the utmost secrecy was necessary...

...Even then, we didn't yet know the exact whereabouts of our targets. We were told that we would have to capture the beach-head, press on to the higher ground and in turn push the Germans back...

...The harbour became a flotilla of ships in preparation for the landings; it quickly filled up with battleships, ships with assault landing craft, motor torpedo craft and every other type of naval vessel you could imagine...

...The day was finally upon us, and we were driven by a security escort for embarkation. I can clearly remember the cheers and call-outs from well-wishers as we went. And by nightfall every ship and vessel had left the south coast and dispatched for Occupied France. Luckily the weather had improved and we were finally on our way.'

'I don't suppose you remember which Normandy beach your regiment landed on?'

I shake my head. 'Getting on that ship is the last memory of my service.'

'But it's more than you recalled before.'

Excitedly, I turn back to Harry. 'That's right, you're right. My memory is finally returning!'

***

Later that night, before turning in, I step out onto the patio once more. The wind is coming in gusts now, and the temperature has dropped considerably.

I gaze up to the heavens; thousands of stars twinkle against the dark sky. My imagination soars and I equate each star with each soldier who left for Normandy more than a year ago and did not return home.

While I stand there staring up into the sky, I am thankful and humble and yet, suddenly, quite alone.

~Chapter 35~

I wake up the next day, pick out a window table in the hotel restaurant and order coffee for breakfast.

Harry rolls in, and joins me at the table a little later. He slumps down in the chair and then rubs his forehead. We initially make some small-talk as the rain pitter-patters against the windows next to us.

'You need some coffee,' I say right off the bat and poured him a cup. 'You appear to be flagging this morning.'

'I ran into 'Shorty' Stevens from my old regiment last night.'

'So, what did you and Shorty get up to?' I ask without a trace of a smile.

'Oh,' he grunts. 'Don't ask.'

'So, this Shorty chap isn't a dry, old stick then?'
'Hardly.'
'Late night, was it?'
'Three o'clock,' he replies.

I nod and go back to my newspaper and flick through each section of The Times (which rustles a bit).

Harry groans.

'What is it?' I ask, looking up.

'The rain, that newspaper…'

'Sorry, but the world's not going to stop on account of your hangover.'

'I don't need it to stop,' he says, 'I just need it to be a bit quieter for a while.'

He sinks his first cup of coffee in one, and forces himself into a stiff-looking, upright seating position as if he is wary of falling back asleep.

In the meantime, as I read, I now make a concentrated effort to turn each page of the newspaper more quietly.

'What are you reading there,' he asks a bit later.

I offer him the newspaper but he bats my offer away. 'My eyes aren't fully working yet.'

'Ah, not quite ready to re-join the world.'

'I'm getting there.'

I have already skimmed the headlines. 'What do you want to know? Politics, business, sport…'

'Politics,' he requests.

'Politics?' I question. 'I didn't take you as a student of government.'

'I'm not usually,' he says, 'but it should wake me up.'

'I see,' I say enlightened. 'Or sober you up?'

I go back and paraphrase the article I have just read. 'Now Churchill is out, Attlee's government is moving ahead with a new social order inspired by the Beveridge Report…'

'A lot of people need help with housing and jobs too,' Harry murmurs. 'That's what we really need, a fresh start.'

I continue, '…the creation of a free medical service: dentists, doctors, hospitals, opticians, pharmacists all under one umbrella. A National Health Service.'

'A free health service for all, indeed.'

'Not one for sufferings that are self-inflicted however,' I tease.

'Very droll. What else?'

'The commentary re-iterates that the country is war-weary. We have given everything - it says - and the government should take care of its people. Churchill was a great war-time leader but we have a different set of challenges now,' I summarise.

'The proof will be in the pudding.' Harry nods philosophically. 'And, talking of food, are you ready to order?'

Talking has made me hungry, so we each order a full English breakfast which we soon polish off, and Harry seems to be revived.

So, we return to a plan of action, which in truth has never been far from my thoughts.

***

'What do we do today?' I ask Harry.

'Carry on where we left off,' he suggests, returning a fixed gaze. 'We know you were here in 1944. Now we have to find out which regiment you belonged to, then we will be able to locate your hometown.'

I shrug. 'Okay.'

Over the next hour or so, we go around the houses, so to speak; back and forth and back again with half-conceived ideas and talk. The coffee comes and goes and is re-filled, cigarettes are lit and smoked and ideas rise up, and then crash and burn.

I take off my jacket, Harry takes off his, and later I put mine back on. I sit back in my chair, sit forward, place my fist under my chin and pull every facial expression you can imagine, from grimaces to expressions of joy (although those quickly dissipate).

'Shall we give them back their table?' I suggest finally. 'At this rate they'll be serving us lunch.'

'We'll go to the lounge,' Harry says, 'and carry on from there.'

We enter the lounge of the hotel; it is decorated sumptuously, how you might imagine the first class to be on board an ocean liner.

We seat ourselves in a quiet corner which overlooks the gardens. After a while, our corner isn't so quiet.

One or two visitors must have overheard details of my dilemma and good-naturedly decide to help. Before long, attracted, possibly, by the noisy chatter, several others start to notice. (The lounge is probably busier than usual because of the bad weather outside; it is still raining cats and dogs).

Suddenly, there is, what I can best describe as, a cocktail party atmosphere and as people enter the lounge, they seem drawn to what they perceive as an informal gathering, a social event of some kind.

It is at first slightly embarrassing but I try to embrace the unusual turn of events, and of course, I am appreciative of their help. Though to be honest, I am a little sceptical as to what it can achieve.

I presume that some of the hotel guests are at a loose end and seeking something to do, and what better way to pass a rainy morning than attempt to solve - or at least guess at - the veracity of someone's missing past.

I'm sure it has the touch of an Agatha Christie mystery for some - without the dead bodies (or skeletons, I hope).

Then Harry informs them, 'There's a girl he's in love with, and he's desperately trying to find.' This adds to the melodrama.

As I survey my new acquaintances, I make a mental note: four soldiers, one demobbed, a businessman, a retired couple, two holiday-makers, an elderly spinster and then we are joined by a vicar on a sabbatical.

After twenty minutes, there are eleven or more, not including Harry and me, either sitting with chairs pulled up next to us, or perched on the ends of, and on, a large settee.

This does not include the bus-boy and waiter who linger after hearing the story of my memory loss (which has to be explained every time a new person joins the group).

There are variations of: 'This man's lost his memory and we're trying to help him get back home.'

'You don't have a strong accent,' notes one soldier. 'You could be from the Home Counties.'

'Possibly you've travelled extensively,' says the vicar, 'and lost your twang.'

'But you're certainly not from up north,' the retiree says. 'I'm from Yorkshire and you have no appreciable accent.'

'Can you speak any languages?' the lady asks.

'I don't know?' I raise my eyes to the ceiling, but nothing comes.

'Here, let me try,' she suggests. 'Comment allez vous?'

I am blank.

'Come estas?'

I shake my head.

'Come sta?'

Nothing.

Then she asks, 'Wie geht es dir?'

Hang on! I understand what she has just asked!

Instinctively I want to reply in German but I am wary of revealing this discovery, so I keep quiet.

You see, the reply: Danke, mir geht es gut (I am fine, thank you) had come to into my head immediately. I wasn't sure how or why I can understand German though…

My mind is in turmoil. I realise that I can speak German and I think I might be fluent. What does it mean?

I glance over to Harry, while squirming in my chair, I maintain a veil of ignorance and no one is the wiser. I shrug apologetically and everyone gives me a sympathetic nod.

'You probably weren't working as a spy either,' she says, 'not knowing German.'

'You may have still travelled,' the holiday-maker says.

'Travelled, doing what though?' I ask. 'If not a spy, how about a cricketer?'

Everyone laughs, because all schoolboys seem to want to be one or the other these days. It handily deflects my earlier discovery.

'May I see your hand?' the bus-boy asks.

I nod, a little perplexed.

The bus-boy takes my hand, studies it and then releases it.

'With respect,' he says, 'your hand is not one of a manual worker. See mine, I have calluses, and blisters and my fingers are raw.'

'I suspect you were a businessman of some sort,' Harry suggests.

Now the businessman joins in intrigued. 'Are you any good at maths?'

'Not particularly, why?'

'Then you're probably not a salesperson either. I have to calculate my sales speedily, work out commissions and percentages…'

I frown which just seems to increase everyone's efforts.

'I've got a question,' a young soldier asks with a smile. 'Who won the F.A. Cup in 1938?'

'Portsmouth,' I reply, quick as a flash.

There is a hushed silence.

'What was the score?'

'4-1, against Huddersfield Town.'

'What does that prove?' Harry asks the private.

'Nothing, really. Probably, he is a football fan, that's all.'

'Or that he might come from Portsmouth,' the vicar suggests, 'and that's why he has managed to remember the event.'

All the guests sit in anticipation, but the idea is quickly scotched when I am able to name the previous ten cup winners too. So, we give up on that line of thought.

'Possibly, you were shipped to Normandy from Portsmouth?' the private asks.

I nod.

'But you can't recall which troop ship you sailed on, or the beach you landed up-on?'

I shake my head.

'And you cannot recall your regiment?'

I shake my head again.

'Can you recall the nickname for them.'

'I can't recall one.'

'I know a few,' he offers. 'Perhaps I could call them out and see if any strike a chord.'

'I'll try,' I promise. I am not sure if it is my imagination or not, but the group seem to lean further forward in expectation.

The private begins reeling off these disparate names and more.

'The Two Tens … The Sweeps … The Para's …the Shropshire Gunners … The Glorious Glosters … The Dorsets …The Springers … The Tigers … The Splashers …'

Sadly, not one strikes a chord in my memory and I can tell their party game is on the wane. The rain outside has stopped and there is even a hint of sunshine.

Frustrated that they aren't able to resolve the puzzle, and as if putting the mystery book down, the guests wish me luck and make their way.

'How long are you here for?' the vicar asks before leaving.

I scratch my head. 'Until I can find Lucy, or I run out of money. Whichever comes first.'

He gives me a generous smile and shakes my hand with his two hands. 'Don't give up. God works in mysterious ways, you know.'

'I hope so,' I say.

'And if that doesn't work,' he says, 'you should consult a medical expert.'

The vicar takes out a small piece of paper with a name and telephone number scribbled on it. 'I'd highly recommend this fellow.'

After he leaves, I sit back down with Harry.

'Coffee?' he suggests.

'I might never want to drink another coffee in my life.' I exclaim. 'But you go ahead.'

'I think you should rest for a while and return at, say, one o'clock for a spot of lunch.'

I smile wearily. 'Thanks.'

I head outside. It is damp underfoot but the sun at last makes an appearance. I walk alone through the gardens of the hotel, wishing I could share the sunshine and the rows of pretty flowers with Lucy.

Then I reflect on my ability to speak German. I translate a few phrases from English to German in my head, and I am surprised how easy it is, giving rise to the question of where I learnt German and why...

~*Chapter 36*~

I join Harry for lunch. We walk down to the harbour to stretch our legs and enjoy the sea air, then stop at nautical-looking pub on the quayside.

The place is extremely busy with so many visitors swelling the ranks of the regulars, and, as we open the door, we are enveloped in the rising noise of their merry-making and happy chatter.

The floor is uneven, the beamed ceiling low, and the cobb walls are covered with an authentic collection of all things nautical: lanterns, mugs and tankards, life-buoys and ships wheels, photographs of old steamers, and nameplates and parts prised from old fishing boats.

We sit down in a cosy nook and sup our beers as we watch a microcosm of the world going on in front our eyes.

Many regulars are propped up at the bar, never too far from the being able to give a shout for their next order. Ex-soldiers, naval personnel, sailors and civilians make up the rest, together with various crew.

Perched on a stool, in front of me is a large, stubbly-faced sea-faring man: captain of a fishing vessel, I presume.

The house's adopted cat wanders through a forest of legs, unconcerned at the general mayhem going on up above.

I see Harry is starting to drift off, his eyes are flickering and we haven't spoken for five minutes.

'Sorry old man, I couldn't get to sleep last night,' he apologizes.

'That's because you didn't go to bed until 3.00 a.m.'

'Well, I'm sorry to say it's caught up with me a bit.'

'I'd never have guessed,' I joke.

As Harry struggles with his sleep-deprivation, I take the opportunity to explore.

At a small, round wooden table across from us, there are a couple of soldiers in full uniform.

Their caps, set on the table by their drinks catch my attention as I had noticed the insignia of the badges.

My eyes are drawn to the design which is oddly familiar: gold garlands frame the keep of a castle and its turrets.

I go over and catch the eye of a soldier. 'Can I have a look at your cap?'

The soldier is a little confused but happily agrees.

I read the Latin motto on the insignia: *Primus in Indis*.

I pick up the cap. 'Which regiment are you?' I ask.

'The First Dorsets.'

'Dorchester?'

'That's where we're based, yes.'

'Thank you.' I go to the bar, and buy two pints of beer and set them down on the soldiers' table.

They look up in surprise.

'They're on me,' I say.

'Thanks.'

'Did you fight in Normandy?' I ask.

'No, in Italy. We were both transferred to the Dorsets.'

'I see.'

'Are you on leave?'

'24 hours. Then returning to base.'

We talk for a while and after my conversation with the two privates, I rouse Harry. I tell him about the familiar-looking cap badges.

Ten minutes later, he suggests that we contact the regiment's headquarters.

We try from the hotel lobby but there is no answer.

'Tomorrow we'll take the train to Dorchester,' he says. 'We'll find out for ourselves.'

~Chapter 37~

We purchase our tickets and catch the south coast train that stops at Dorchester.

We pass through some pretty English villages, making frequent stops: Christchurch, Pokesdown, Branksome, Parkstone and Hamworthy.

Normality in England - at least on the surface - has returned. As I gaze out, people are smiling, walking their dogs, running errands and chatting across garden fences - all without fear. Fear of falling bombs, losing loved ones, and the worry of not having enough food to put on the table. I watch this more optimistic world from my compartment window for a while.

I study the greens and browns of the landscape and it seems familiar, but the motion of the train and the sunshine that streams through the window soon makes me sleepy.

I sit back and briefly glance over to Harry before closing my eyes.

I want to think of Lucy, or dream about a fable, or a beautiful resort as one might do before drifting off to sleep, but a different memory returns to my consciousness, and in contrast to those desires it is darker and more menacing.

As I recall the memory from my past, I am restless; I fidget and kick out my feet.

I hear Harry utter something like, 'Settle down old man,' and 'It's okay, you must be dreaming.'

But I am not dreaming, at least not at first.

My flashbulb memory continues for some time and I fall into a semi-sleep. Suddenly, I open my eyes - and much to Harry's surprise - I stand up.

'What is it?' Harry asks.

He calls out my name but I am temporarily detached from reality and I barely hear him.

The train is approaching a station and is beginning to slow. Lost in my reverie, however, I open the door to the carriage and jump directly from the train.

Harry watches it all, incredulous, before he lunges over to the door.

'What the hell are you thinking?' he calls out to me, as the train door is still swinging back and forth on its hinges. 'We're not there yet!'

The hard landing shakes me out of my earlier state.

I view Harry as he and the train recedes and he becomes smaller and smaller until he is gone altogether.

Poor Harry - having to deal with me and my problems. I wonder if my amnesia is getting worse, or if there is something more playing with my mind.

Lying there on the grassy embankment, I experience a sharp pain in my ankle. I have taken a bad fall and twisted my foot.

And as for thinking, I'm not. I have jumped instinctively just as I remember doing so once before.

None of it makes sense, even to me at this moment. All I know is that my ankle is on fire with the pain.

After a while, I presume the train has stopped at the next station, but I can no longer see it. A few minutes later, from around the curve of the track, Harry appears, awkwardly, half-jogging and half-shuffling his way back to me.

'I think you'll be for it!' he says gravely, as soon as he reaches me. 'You might even be barred from this line if they catch you.'

He then aims some choice swear words at me and my stupid actions.

I ignore Harry's fretting and try to stand up, but as soon as I put pressure on my right foot, I grimace in pain.

'Come on,' Harry urges and considers our options. 'Quick. There's a signal box further up the track. Do you think you can get there?'

I ignore his suggestion.

I go off, hobbling in the other direction until the pain forces me to stop.

'What are you doing?' he calls after me.' Have you lost your senses?'

Harry catches up and I finally accept his offer of physical support, so that I can take the weight off my injured foot. I still do not want to turn around however, but I realise I have no choice.

'If you want me to help, we need to go the other way.'

I reluctantly agree.

'You are acting odd,' Harry says, 'not like your old-self at all.'

We continue until we reach the signal box. Harry taps on the door and a railway worker comes to help. I am taken into the small hut and offered a seat. I see his name stitched on his jacket.

'Thanks for your help, Sidney,' I say, grimacing.

'Call me Sid,' he says.

I collapse into the chair and immediately I pull off my shoe and sock. My foot is swelling up by the minute.

'How is it?' Harry asks, still in shock at recent events.

'Fine,' I lie.

Sid inspects my foot and expresses what I have already feared.

'It could be broken.'

'I think it's just swollen, a bit of rest and I'll be fine,' I reassure Sid and then Harry.

The two of them question my prognosis and insist I have it checked out. Sid points to a truck.

'I can take you if you like,' he offers.

'To where?'

'The hospital!' Harry says. 'Can you make it to the truck?'

I nod, and soon after, he is driving Harry and me to the local hospital.

'Won't they miss you?' I ask Sid as we leave.

'Not for an hour.'

I start to wonder if a catastrophe of some sort might happen if he isn't back in time…

Soon, we are in a small hospital in the heart of the rural countryside. Harry helps me to the door, finds a wheelchair, and pushes me from there.

I give a wave of thanks to Sid as he leaves.

'Please wait over there,' the receptionist instructs. Harry dutifully pushes me to the waiting area. I can tell he is disappointed in me.

When drinking, Harry will laugh off such things. But he hasn't been drinking and he does not laugh it off.

Harry soon lights into me, albeit in a hissed whisper, presumably in respect for being in a hospital.

'What were you thinking?' he asks.

I frown. 'I wasn't.'

'Why did you do that?'

'I recalled jumping from a train before.'

'Well, that explains it all then!' he scoffs. 'I thought we were getting somewhere - now this!'

'I can explain.'

'Really?' He crosses his arms.

'I had a flashbulb memory. I was literally re-enacting a memory, although I didn't know it, until it was too late.'

'So, this memory involved jumping off a moving train, did it?'

'Unfortunately, it did.'

Harry slaps me on the back and forces a laugh although he is still shaking his head.

'Well, you're still in one piece. I suppose we should be thankful for that.' He looks me in the eye. 'Let's hear about it then.'

I glance at the receptionist and then back to Harry.

'Do you remember I told you I was on a train when the German fighters dropped their bombs on my village?'

Harry nods. 'What about it?'

'The memory I had on the train felt amazingly real, as though I was living through it again.'

'So real, that you stepped off the train?'

I nod and share my memory.

The train slows as soldiers jostle to see out of the windows. I push my way to a door.

'What the hell are you doing?' a soldier shouts as I open it.

'I have to go back,' I shout.

'You'll be court-martialled and thrown in prison!'

'I'm not deserting, just helping. I'll make it to camp in plenty of time before we sail.'

'We have our orders!'

'Please cover for me.'

With that I clamber onto the door ledge and when the train slows, I throw off my gear and jump from the moving train.

I take a hard fall onto the grassy embankment, my equipment scattered everywhere.

I look up to see the last of the bombers in retreat and then over towards the village to see the rising smoke. I have to go back to my fiancée, to see if she is okay, alive…

I pick up my steel helmet, my ammunition pouches, my rifle, my haversack and kitbag.

I make my way back, hugging the side of the railway line. Finally, I find Lucy, she is alive and unharmed.'

Harry just listens with an open-mouth and then shakes his head. 'So, you went back for Lucy?'

I nod.

'You must really love this girl.'

'I do.'

'Well, we're not giving up yet,' he encourages. 'But look at the state of you; we need to get you fixed up first.'

I am admitted and examined, bandaged and sent on my way, 'Keep your foot elevated,' the nurse says as we leave.

'It's late,' I say to Harry.

'I think you've had enough excitement for one day,' Harry teases. 'There must be a bed and breakfast where we can stay the night.'

~Chapter 38~

St James Hospital, Wareham

The following morning a newly-arrived nurse at the hospital is having her usual morning tea break in the refectory when she overhears a colleague telling a story to the sister.

Apparently, the nurse (telling the story) has attended to a young man who has recently come in with a suspected broken ankle. The man's ankle has been bandaged up, and is not broken; he has severe bruising and ligament damage.

Sister asks, 'What caused it?'

'I heard that he jumped from a moving train.'

The 'new' nurse, the one who has only been half-listening, sits up now.

'What did he do after that?' Sister asks.

The nurse shrugs. 'He hobbled alongside the track.'

'Which way did he go?' the new nurse interrupts.

Sister and nurse both look along the table in surprise. The story-telling nurse utters, 'What a funny thing to ask.'

'Was it towards the village?' the new nurse asks again.

The nurse smiles uncertainly. 'How on earth should I know?'

'What was his name?'

'I really don't know. Why?'

'Oh.' She shakes her head. 'No reason.'

Directly after that, the new-nurse leaves.

'How odd!' Sister and her colleague exclaim.

~Chapter 39~

We stay at a local bed and breakfast for the evening in Wareham, Dorset. It is almost full, so we share a room with twin beds.

Harry isn't someone you would naturally volunteer to room with, what with his penchant for getting up every couple of hours, making himself a drink and then trying to sleep again. Failing that, he let himself out and walks around the block.

I am not sure if he is an insomniac or has troubling recollections that keep him awake at night. Then I think about his missing leg and how little he makes of it.

Whatever it is, (and he never has said) as hard as he tries to be quiet, he is always crashing into something or knocking something over. Often during the wee hours, I hear him apologise and say, 'Sorry about that,' or 'Go back to sleep, old man.'

So, now I know why Harry's afternoon kip is so important to him. Anyway, the room is cheap but comfortable, basic yet friendly.

In the morning, we are one of the first to arrive in the dining room. I am able to borrow a walking stick which helps me be more independent.

We enjoy a breakfast of bacon rashers and eggs. I pick up a copy of the Times as Harry strikes up a conversation with an attractive young lady on the next table.

'Travelling very far?' Harry asks her.

'I'm walking the South Downs with my friend.'

Harry now notices the empty seat.

The woman smiles. 'She's a slow starter in the morning; she's still getting ready.'

'I've always wanted to do something like that.'

The woman smiles again. 'Have a leisurely start to the day - or walk the South Downs?'

'Oh, I see.' Harry laughs. 'The walk I meant.'

'Come along if you like,' she offers. 'It's very informal.'

'I wish I could.' Harry turns to me and bites his lip. 'You see, we're on a bit of a mission.'

'That sounds intriguing…'

Harry proceeds to explain my situation, something I am getting quite used to, and every so often I am somewhat obliged to feign nods and give the appropriate expressions from behind the newspaper. Much sympathy is thrown my way.

When we are onto our coffee, the woman's friend finally makes an appearance.

The newcomer seems to catch Harry's eye and I can see his mind working, or rather clunking away, in the way that it usually does; two boys and two girls…

Fortunately for me, the first lady puts a stop to any such notions and tells my story to her friend. The earlier reactions are repeated, and more sympathy and more incredulity follow.

Harry fawns over the two of them for the remaining duration (or two cups of tea), after which we make our way and set off through the villages towards Dorchester. It is mid-morning by this time.

***

As we come into one particular village called Wool, I peek beyond the trees, through the broken clouds and to a church spire in the distance. I feel something; it is hard to explain: a sort of shiver travels up and down my spine, a spasm of sorts that seems to wash over me. Whatever it is, a powerful sensation has grabbed me.

'Stop!' I call out to the driver.

'What is it?' Harry asks in surprise.

'This seems familiar.'

'Does it? Do you recognise something perhaps?'

I nod and then tap on the driver's shoulder. 'Drop us off here please.'

Harry kindly pays the fare and I limp off, walking cane in hand.

'What is it?' Harry asks, shuffling up next to me.

'I know this road,' I say. 'I'm sure of it.'

As I look more closely, it is as if the gates to my memory are slowly opening, a trickle at first, then a steady flow of past experiences.

I can only guess what a blind person experiences when they are able to see for the first time. For me, my life experiences begin to flood back into my head. Where there have been blank, dark recesses, there is now light pouring in.

I walk along a terraced street, pausing outside one house and see a sloping roof, a chimney pot blackened by soot and a well-kept front garden; a house squeezed in between countless others. All seem familiar.

'Is that it?' Harry asks. 'Is that your old home?'

'No,' I shake my head. 'But it has significance of some kind.'

I turn hesitantly back to Harry. I am anxious, excited and impatient, all at once.

'You're all right,' Harry encourages. 'You go ahead, old man. I'll follow in your footsteps just behind you.'

I slowly make my way up to one particular entrance in the row of houses; I undo the latch on the gate and then push it open.

'That badly needs some oil,' Harry laughs.

I stop, irritated, because I am distracted from untangling these newly-arrived memories.

Harry throws up his hands. 'Sorry - don't mind me, carry on.'

I do not say anything; I have these other thoughts swimming around my mind, some more focussed than others.

I walk along the road a bit further. On my left is a tobacconist just like the one I have remembered over and over again.

A little dizzy now, I go in, as Harry skulks outside.

'Good morning.' A pear-shaped woman greets me.

I take it all in. The numerous jars of sweets lined up on the shelves, catch my eye. My gaze returns to the old wooden counter and a large register that sits atop of it.

The shop-keeper stands there, patient but expectant.

'Can I have a packet of tobacco,' I ask, purely out of politeness.

'Yes, of course.'

The lady measures the amount and rings it up.

'Does an elderly man still work here?' I ask as I go to pay her.

'Mr Thompson?'

'Yes, I think so, that could be him.'

'He's retired. When I moved here, I took over the shop.'

'I see.'

I cast my eyes around the little shop one more time, and once again, there is a familiarity to everything.

I thank the proprietor and leave.

'Any luck?' Harry asks a moment later.

'I'm not fully sure,' I say. 'It's like walking into a dream.'

I walk on and Harry, bless him, follows me with no idea as to where we are headed next. What a friend he is.

'But you do recognise it?' Harry asks again a moment later.

Frustratingly for him, I still do not answer, but it is not out of impoliteness. I am worried my newly-found memory might disappear if I do not give it my full concentration.

I arrive at the High Street now, and glance up and down.

Without thinking, or the slightest hesitation, I make my way along a twisting, tree-lined road that leads to a railway station.

A little time after, I stop across from the station. I see a white trellis fence and the war memorial in all its glory; a monument to fallen soldiers of the First World War. I glance at the names inscribed on the memorial, observing the manicured grass and the neat rows of flowers set out, with such love and care.

Harry is wide-eyed now. 'Well even I remember this,' he says. 'It's just as you described!'

I smile and move on along the footpath leading to the entrance, and as I do, I then catch sight of 'The Station

Café'. I am taken aback at my initial sighting and unexpectedly my heart lifts.

In the window of the café, I notice a woman standing with her back turned to me. She wears a long, flowing dress that is colourful and stylish and shimmers in the light, as if made from silk. I am immediately reminded of Paris and the shows there that might display something quite so lovely.

The dress accentuates her figure. Her hair is radiant and her chestnut curls tumble down to her neckline.

I motion with my palm to Harry to remain where he is, because I do not need his help anymore…but first I go over to thank Harry with a handshake.

A mere handshake - for what Harry has done - seems wholly inadequate, so I give him a hug.

Harry is surprised because this is probably the last thing he is expecting.

'What's all that about?' he asks.

'A show of my gratitude that's all. I want to thank you for your friendship.'

He waves my appreciation away. 'You'd do the same for me, old man.'

'But you've helped me more than necessary and more than I could have ever expected.'

For once Harry is speechless.

'Here,' I say. 'Hang on to this.'

I pass my walking cane to Harry. 'I have to stand up on my own two feet,' I joke. In truth, I have recalled the comment Lucy has written in her diary about me 'standing on my own two feet'.

I do not want to disappoint her.

'Good luck!' Harry calls out after me, beaming, he appears to be as happy as I am.

Once through the door, my ankle is throbbing, but I do not care.

I walk haltingly towards the woman in the café, until I am close enough to smell her perfume. I stand there for a moment and hope and pray it isn't a cruel dream - and I am not back in my quarters, dozing off on the train or in a hospital again.

The woman does not know I am there - or perhaps she does - but I gently touch - or rather caress - the back of her arm. Slowly, she turns around, as if in a repeat of my flashbulb memory. Of course, this time, I see her full face... It is Lucy...

Strangely, she shows no surprise. She gazes into my eyes, then smiles, and takes my hand in hers. We embrace. And as I stand here, lost in this miraculous moment, my heart is no longer empty but full of love, happiness, and joy.

'Oh, Jack. You remembered,' she says and touches my face as we embrace again. 'I always knew that one day you would remember and come back here.'

'Of course, I always wanted to come back,' I smile. 'But back to you.'

'But you chose me...'

'Lucy darling, it's always been you.'

In some ways I have gone back in time, before I went off to Normandy, before we parted. Yet, standing here, I am not thinking of the past, or of the uncertain future, just the present, and how wonderful it feels.

If my mind is playing tricks on me, I do not care. Somehow the time, the months and years have connected again and everything is just as it was, my memory has returned and most importantly I have found my angel, my Lucy.

~Chapter 40~

August 1st, 2007

I am sitting out in the garden, bathed in sunshine, trying to navigate my way around my laptop computer with a poor internet connection. After a while I give up.

I push the laptop aside, pick up a newspaper and skim across some articles. I sit back. An article has prompted me to think of my days at Oxford University, when I had studied foreign languages.

As it has turned out, my German course came in very handy indeed. I worked in a couple of special operations for what was codenamed: Bodyguard (what is now known as the general operation created to deceive German Intelligence). I did some translations for them back in

1943. That was all there was to it. I suppose Harry wasn't too far off when he speculated about the 'Oxford type' visitor who came looking for me.

And as for Harry, he still lives in Bournemouth, although frail, you often find him having a drink in the Kings Head.

He hasn't lost his charm, but he never did settle down. We meet up from time to time, and I still count him as my very dearest friend.

My great grand-daughter joins me.

'Happy Anniversary, Grandad.'

'Thank you,' I smile, and give my great granddaughter, Erin, a hug.

She sits down and her big eyes look up at me.

'Can you tell me the story of how you and grandma met?'

'Well,' I recall, 'it was a long time ago but the first time I met her I gave her a ride on my bicycle. We used to live on the same street, you see.'

'How old were you?'

'Oh, about your age: six or seven years old, I suppose.'

'Then you went to war and forgot about her.'

'That was many years later.' I smile wistfully. 'I couldn't remember her because I had lost my memory.'

'But your memory is better now.'

I give a laugh. 'My short-term memory is going, but I remember everything else quite vividly now.'

'Then you found Grandma again.'

'Actually, she found me - in hospital - and then she took care of me.'

'That's when your memory returned?'

'Not for a while after.' I nod. 'But it did eventually.'

'Then you texted her?'

I laugh and shake my head. 'We couldn't text back then.'

'Please,' she begs in the way a child sometimes does. 'Tell me some more.'

'Well, in those days you couldn't just text or email someone in order to contact them… but I returned home and I was able to find her by retracing my footsteps. Fortunately, she was there already waiting for me, where I remembered last seeing her.'

'Then you got married?'

'Less than a year later, we did.'

'How many years ago was it?'

'60 years today,' I say and a tear comes to my eye.

'Sorry, grandad, I didn't mean to make you sad.'

I try not to well up. 'But I'm not sad; I'm just a having a moment of nostalgia, there's a difference.'

'What are you two talking about?' Lucy comes by with two glasses of home-made lemonade. She places them down.

I give my great grand-daughter a little nudge in the ribs as if to say: watch this.

'I was saying how lucky I am to have met you all those years ago.'

Lucy puts her hands on her hips.

'Flattery will get you nowhere,' she says.

I smile. 'You can't blame a fellow for trying.'

'Yes, you were always trying.' Lucy laughs and comes over and gives me a kiss and a cuddle.

'See that,' I say turning to Erin. 'I always knew it might work one day!'

I sit there for a moment or two after Lucy and Erin go off together.

For some reason, a thought comes, seemingly from somewhere and nowhere.

I recall the conversation between Lucy and me at the Lyons Tea House in Bournemouth all of those years ago.

We had shared with each other our hopes for the future, and the waiter had dropped his tray - much to our astonishment at the time.

Well, there was something remarkable about the timing of this occurrence that I have never been able to forget. Possibly, I read too much into it, but Lucy felt it too, I know she had.

Was it synchronicity of some sort, or just a waiter being clumsy?

Whatever it was, I realise that we have in fact loved each other, and grown old together… just as I had wished… and just as Lucy had wanted, too.

Sitting there, that day, at that precise moment, I was to learn that we had made the same exact wish too.

The End

Period/British English Word Help

Chapter 4

Scrumping: to steal fruit from an orchard or garden (often a boyhood pastime).

Chapter 6

W.A.A.F.: Women's Auxiliary Air Force.

Chapter 9

Coffin nails: Cigarettes
Kip: Sleep
Red Ink: Red wine
Dry, old stick: Dull and boring with nothing much to say

Chapter 10

What's your poison? What would you like to drink? (Usually alcoholic).

Chapter 11

Wet my whistle: To consume a beverage
Best of British: An expression of good luck.
Ticker: Heart.

Chapter 12

Three sheets to the wind: Inebriated; when the three ropes of a ship's sail were loose in the wind the sail would flop about in a 'drunken' fashion.

Florin: Two Shilling coin
Brolly: Umbrella

Chapter 14

R.A.F. Royal Air Force.

Chapter 16

In the soup: In trouble.
Bally: An old-fashioned euphemism for 'bloody'.

Chapter 34

Plonk: Wine

General Information

Chapter 1

Idoform is a compound of iodine and has antiseptic properties, so was used as a cleaning disinfectant in the wards and as an antiseptic for wounds etc.

Chapter 2

Penicillin was mass produced in Europe in July 1943.

Chapter 10

'Bless 'em all' (the long, and the short and the tall): A song believed to have originated from the First World War but was made popular in the Second World War by the likes of Gracie Fields, Vera Lynn and George Fornby; essentially a homage to allied serviceman.

Chapter 12

V-E Day (sometimes known as 'VE DAY' or 'V DAY') Victory in Europe Day; a public holiday marking the surrender of Nazi Germany and the unconditional surrender of its armed forces marking the end of WW11 in Europe.

Printed in Great Britain
by Amazon